The Only Living Girl in Chicago

THE ONLY LIVING GIRL
IN CHICAGO

by Mallory Smart

Trident Press
Boulder, CO

ISBN: 978-1-951226-12-1

Cover art by Dmitry Samarov

Published by Trident Press
940 Pearl St.
Boulder, CO 80302

tridentcafe.com/trident-press-titles

To the ones we lost and things we dreamed and what we wished we could still remember.

Enter John and the Rhinoceros

Halfway through Eugène Ionesco's 1959 absurdist play "Rhinoceros" she began to think of John. She always thought of him late at night when she was smoking and reading things that were weird, full of melancholy and trauma.

She made herself a cup of black coffee. It was Stumptown blend from when she was in Portland for a poetry reading. She was originally hesitant to buy the coffee beans because she foolishly worried that it wouldn't get by security, but it had. When she told this to her friend later, he laughed and said they don't care about food they only care about liquids.

That didn't help and only made her feel dumb.

At this point as the narrator, I should mention that this friend is not John. John is dead. This makes her sad to think about and I guess that's why she was thinking about him while reading a sad play on her Chicago rooftop.

She sipped her coffee and smoked while looking out at the dim skyline that she could see from her building. The crisscrossing of styles and shapes of all that surrounded her made her just think that what was once distinct about this place was now a thing of the past. When she saw the skyscrapers surrounded in a loop by buildings from the 19th century, the overlap of intellectual and aesthetic integrity seemed gone. She wanted to feel so fulfilled by all the good that was happening in her life, but she just couldn't at that point.

So many people in her life had died but this one really hit her for some reason.

She went onto Twitter so that she could look through their old DMs.

She wondered if there would ever be a time where Twitter would realize that he was gone forever and just delete his account and then all their interactions would be lost.

She immediately highlighted all their messages and copied them into her notes app on her iPhone. This process took a while because it takes a while to load each page as you scroll up and they had literal years of messages.

When she pasted it into the notes app it showed his Twitter profile image, and it made her laugh. It was such a clumsy brand he tried to throw together but he was still the best writer she had ever met. She dropped her cigarette in her coffee and went to bed wondering if she would ever meet anyone like that again.

Somewhere Not Here

Somewhere, not here, she was on her computer thinking about how to go about her day. Her name was Zoe.

She dwelled on her life and her relationships:

Go-to friend: Tyler

Boyfriend: Brad

Crush: Riley

Guy who hits on her: Liam

Guy who won't leave her alone online: Joe (not really but just go with it)

Her coffee buddy who loves *Twin Peaks*: she called him "Cooper" for fun

and so on...

She wanted to see if there was some kind of weird common thread amongst them all, but she could only find the love and support that they all showed her. Fucked up right?

She so casually dissed so many of them but they would go to great lengths to help her through life.

Be her 2 AM ride or die people.

People were important.

One of her people had died recently so now she didn't think of him.

Another one of her people became someone who would never be her people again. It all weighed on her.

So now she just sat down in San Francisco and questioned her purpose.

For 10 years she had been doing little other than be a quirky human who wanted to pursue art but now, getting harshly close to her 30s, she decided the jig was up and shit had to get serious now and change.

Amen, right?

Also, wtf close to 30 is terrifying...let's all hope she gets her shit together because after 30 you only have death.

She began to make a list of things she currently loved, things she wanted to have done in the next five years, and things she needed to have done before she died.

Here is that list for the next five years:

  -meet David Lynch and play video games for 12 hours

  -hide communist propaganda in all the aisles in all Targets in all the world

  -sit at a park with a typewriter and pretend that that was an original idea

  -hit up all 50 states without thinking about death in all of them

-meet every single online friend before they reach their untimely end which is becoming a somewhat fucked up thing now

-get wildly drunk and not get hung-over

-magically learn how to play guitar and wow Sarah Paulson with her amazing guitar playing skills (why not?)

-become a rock star, director, actress, and professor and then complain about how it's hurting her identity as a writer

-actually, be a writer

She sighed with relief that she got that all out. Now she could go and make some coffee and pretend she did something real with her day.

Watching *Twin Peaks* didn't count.

It Be Like That Sometimes...

It started thundering a bit from a dark empty sky as Tyler, in Chicago, began messaging her. He was maybe 3000 miles away or some shit like that.

He walked toward Lincoln Park to grab a coffee at the only 24hr Starbucks in the city.

He committed himself to not looking up as he stared at his iPhone with a kind of trust as he walked to the Starbucks.

It sat beneath a comedy theatre that once housed renowned cast members from *SNL* like Chris Farley and Tina Fey.

He found this sort of interesting but not that interesting. He never went up to see a show even though his friends constantly invited him. He thought of the time, three years earlier, when his sort of friend, Peter, invited him to watch Improv at Pipers Alley on a cold day in February, not so much for any reason but to occupy his mind as he walked, though his conversation with her was something else on his mind.

Almost a block away he began to feel more like he was in Oakland than in Chicago.

He looked up with soft eyes, and thought of where Zoe was now, over 3000 miles away.

She, in Oakland, came in and out of the conversation as she sat with her cat eating Chinese food. Their texting felt like a gentle, shapeless dance and that killed him.

It killed her too.

She stroked her small grey cat's fur thoughtfully as she waited for him to ask her about her day. He always did but tonight he was late. Instead, she decided to ask her cat, Minion, about her day but that bitch clearly had no fucks to give. She threw on Netflix to keep her company since the cat gave her none.

"How are yoooooo," he finally messaged her. He knew those kind of half assed "hellos" kind of bugged her but he did it anyways.

She was passively watching Don Draper stare painfully at something or other when her phone chimed.

She typed back, "On the couch trying to fall asleep. You?"

"Not talking to people at Starbucks"

"Yeah, it be like that sometimes..."

They continued messaging each other in a kind of weak and overcome way. She sat in alone in her Oakland apartment, aware of the purposelessness of their conversation. She looked distractedly at her TV and then her phone, not sure of when she would lazily stop looking or when he would suddenly stop responding, and eventually one of them did.

She sat there, silently, for a few minutes, staring at her phone with a lack of object permanence.

Her phone chimed one more time.

"Have you ever thought what it would feel like to self-defenestrate?" he asked.

She turned her phone on silent and went to sleep. There wasn't enough coffee in the world that would make that conversation worth staying awake for.

Looking Forward to Not Dying and Shit

The mornings were always the same. A vibe of disconnect and displacement. Not always sure where she was or why. This morning began with Zoe typing. She pressed her fingers on a qwerty keyboard with cohesive precision and rhythm. But her thoughts were not precise. Tyler came online and filled up the empty space that had earlier been occupied by sex chats and Netflix. Tyler said 'hello'. Tyler said 'how are you' and waited for a response.

She took a stodgy gulp from her Mighty Mango Naked Juice and their messages on Facebook started from there:

Zoe Clark: Still in bed. Woke up like 20 min ago

Tyler Kiosk: So, you're in the same mess I'm in

Zoe Clark: Yes

Zoe Clark: I couldn't fall asleep last night

Tyler Kiosk: Same

Zoe Clark: Maybe I shouldn't have watched American Horror Story all night

Tyler Kiosk: Probably

Tyler Kiosk: I need coffee

Zoe Clark: Same

Zoe Clark: What'd you end doing last night?

Tyler Kiosk: Nothing. Just played Limbo...

Zoe Clark: Fun stuff

Tyler Kiosk: It's a chill game. No real purpose other than to just experience it and move forward. It feels very Tim Burton. I think you'd like it.

Zoe Clark: Cool

Tyler Kiosk: Yeah

Tyler Kiosk: Hey if you want to watch the meteor shower tonite just message me and we'll FaceTime

Zoe Clark: Yeah maybe. I'm not sure how that will work with LA time vs Chicago time. I'll let you know later. I gotta get to work

Tyler Kiosk: K

Zoe pushed herself back from the MacBook and shut it. She grabbed her backpack and ran to the BART station across from the theatre. Oakland sucked. Her life sucked too. She squinted at the sun while waiting at the platform, knowing that she was going to be late for work again. The sun through the fog created a spotlight on what used to be a "Cash for Gold" and was now a "Vapor Haus", a den for douchebags and men in their 30s wearing fedoras bitching about women on the internet. It seemed like all these businesses and trends just came and went with the seasons. She began to wonder what ever happened to hookah lounges and oxygen bars and what they even served at oxygen bars, but the train came before her thought could find any real meaning. She grabbed a seat and put her earphones in. This was her life now. She was a 30-year-old who listened to Mac Demarco on the train.

Getting to her sad office job in San Francisco involved a 30-minute ride on the BART, a trolley, a bus, and a complete detachment of self. But the rates were still cheaper than the gas prices and toll to get across the Bridge. Zoe had accepted that these daily trips were necessary, but not enough to make the words "obsolete" and "futile" drift from her mind as "Salad Days" rattled her eardrums. On her way to the office, she repositioned her earphone three times and took them out just to smell how much ear wax she had gotten on them once. She stuck her finger in her ear and examined it before putting the ear bud back in and thought about how she really needed to get those ear swab things her parents would stock in the linen closet next to the bathroom at home.

Zoe reached her hand into the pocket of her skinny jeans and fished out her iPhone 6. She wrote a note that simply said, "ear swab things" and then thought again and added the words "toilet paper" before putting it back in her front pocket.

She thought of how she had gotten there. Wondered if it was too late to make a change this far into her 20's and took stock of whether she really had grown all that much from the skinny, gawky girl she had once been years ago.

"Work is a waste of space and mental energy," Tyler, who Zoe had known since high school, told her last night via email. "We warehouse our past selves because we cannot accept what we have become and so we" — he did not mean we — "use nostalgia as a safety net when really it's quicksand. You've gotta just let stuff go, Zoe."

Tyler was an awkward, pale ginger. But he had been working ferociously these past few years to kill the person he was.

"It's sad because it signifies how our entire lives have become currency in the capitalist marketplace, "he messaged even more later.

Zoe slept with her Russian boyfriend on an Indian rug made by slaves and paid rent in cultural capital by manipulating digital images and making them art.

"By contributing to the financial mayhem there in San Francisco, you're giving up ownership of your own life, and taking away the ownership from others. You might as well be one of those corporate start-up douchebags here in the back here in the Loop. What happened to you China? You used to be cool."

This made her laugh, they always managed to finesse Simpson's quotes into their conversations. Even the serious ones: Season 7, episode 4. It was just one of their many things.

None of this conversation made sense, but if you knew them it would. Friends for over 10 years now separated by a huge swath of time and space, they had basically created a language of their own. He hated her for abandoning him in Chicago so she could move to San Francisco two years ago. She hated him for never letting that go.

San Francisco two years ago was a different place. Now, things had changed. Now, the people of San Francisco began to think that everyone who was moving in was a degenerate. It was also the year that Zoe would quit her job. The city became occupied by online people. Blue people. Hoodie wearing people. Flip flop people. White, glasses wearing people. Asian people. Indian people. Even bro people. The people were coming, and the city didn't like it. The people didn't trust the online types and why would they, every degenerate a Guy Fawkes mask with a floating question mark above it. Only two years before, those online types came and saw and occupied and made everyone uncomfortable and left. The San Franciscans even began to suspect that the Internet itself was degenerate. A sort of malware created by Al Gore and Putin that would take away their hot dogs and Miley Cyrus. Yes, even the Internet itself was degenerate. The Internet could be around at any time and any place. Maybe even in their hand. It was communist for sure. And it would go on their YouTube and turn it in RedTube. And they would take their phone in their hands and look up RedTube and know that the internet was degenerate for sure.

So, the San Franciscans began to leave San Francisco. And all who stayed, adapted to the new way of life. Zoe just could never decide whether she could. She wasn't a San Franciscan. But she wasn't really a Chicagoan anymore either. She was just in stuck in stasis with no true feeling of object permanence. If that was even something she could feel.

She sat in front of her Mac and thought of the bog and the rain. It's why she wanted to move to San Francisco in the first place.

"CAHL-E-FOUR-KNEE-UHHH", she dragged the word out in her head. Rolled it around until it sounded like it had come straight from the lips of Arnold Schwarzenegger to her brain. Until the mere thought of the place had morphed into scenes from the *Terminator* and *Terminator Two*.

She continued to think of California the place and not California the idea. Not the California seen on TV where everyone wore Ray-Bans, although everyone actually did. But California, the Instagram filter of escape. A sepia tone-wrapped idea almost tangible, like it was actually tied to the dirt and the air. It was a land of vast beginnings. And San Francisco was a city built on precarious symmetries. Symmetries that melded and clashed and morphed themselves into something beautiful and earthy. Fuckbois and poets met. Eggrolls and burritos joined hands. Computers and trees created mandates for the world to live in. Palo Alto to the south. Yosemite to the east. Palo Alto had been inching it's way closer to San Francisco for some time. 19 yr. old millionaires had started coming in from the hills to buy up houses. Real estate prices spiked. Start-ups started popping up in the city to cut down on commutes. So the degenerates wouldn't have to drive an hour to work. She saw it all. She saw the first wave of people leave. She saw her favorite burrito go up from $4.50 to $8 and she saw the Asian family who made her favorite eggroll pack up and go.

People need to work. Without work people don't get money. Without money they can't eat, they can't live, and they certainly can't pay rent. If they can't pay rent, they lose their shitty homes that are close to work. Without shitty homes close to work she can't eat, she can't live, and she can't pay rent.

Her life sucked.

Before going to sleep she made another list of things she needed that her parents would've had back home like Suave Shampoo or those pink Bic razors.

Zoe didn't have those kind of things at her house. If you could call it a house. But that's what you call if when you're 30 and living 3000 miles away from your mom and dad—a home. You need to call it a home when you're at that age where your Facebook feed is no longer clogged with pictures of keg-stands but of babies. When the men you used to date now wear ties and deal with noxious things like human resources. When the women you used to fuck are now married to men and are pregnant and you always knew they'd go back to men, but you didn't want to say anything after the fact because that would make you sound bitter and you totally aren't bitter what the fuck do you have to bitter about its not like you still care.

Yes, you need to call it a home. Even if your home is just a bed in a loft shared with four other girls, separated into rooms via laundry baskets, bed sheets, and a Billy bookshelf from Ikea.

She hadn't been home for quite some time. The last few months were spent hopping from city to city reciting poetry on the weekends and crashing at her boyfriend's place during the week. She had a drawer there devoted to her few belongings, and a bathroom that was shared with three other dudes. A bathroom that had a sink plastered in dried up toothpaste with hair shavings stuck to it like it was glue and the mixed odor of Axe body spray and Old Spice. A bathroom that was horrifyingly messy, was something that brought the word Fallujah to mind every time she thought about it, was stocked with all things a bathroom must have. Dave's mom liked to send care packages along with money. But now her and Dave were no longer "her and Dave". And now when she ordered from the new Chinese place down the street, she got two eggrolls instead of four. Now she had returned to the place that she had been paying rent for the whole time. Nothing had changed necessarily. Her things were left untouched. Her cat still hid in the same place in her closet and iPhone charger was still right next to her bed, but it still felt like a new place entirely. When she had finally gotten around to restocking her own bathroom, she had only thought to buy the staples like shampoo and leave-in conditioner from Whole Foods. She wasn't sure if Whole Foods even had ear swab things like she noted before. But she knew she had to have them. Or buy new Apple earbuds.

The next morning, Zoe made it into her office at 9:15 am and settled into her tiny 4x4 cubicle. She turned on the computer in front of her and pretended to work while she ate noodles out of a cup. She looked out her window at the old factory across the street that was now a startup better than the one she worked at. It made some dating app that allowed two strangers at a bar to hit on each other without having to talk to them or buy them a drink. Just a bunch of single people in a bar texting each other in hopes of finding someone they could text in other places alone. Zoe wished she worked there instead. And then she wished she didn't really work at all. She wished she could live in San Francisco and actually afford to just be a writer. But San Francisco was no longer a place for writers. So she worked at a start-up during the day and she worked as a writer at night.

When the workday was over, Zoe went home to her apartment.

"How the fuck did I get here," Zoe thought while throwing off her shoes. She only got to this city two years ago and she still couldn't shake the strange feeling of it all. There was something dank about San Francisco that wasn't present back home in Chicago, which is interesting given that Chicago was built on swampland.

She shook off all those second thoughts and looked for the only being that made her happy these days. A small squirrelly cat that would jump out from the closet to each day to greet her. Thank god cats love small spaces. Her living arrangement was perfect for a creature like that.

"MINION," she shouted in a gleeful yet horribly impersonated voice as she picked the mangy ball of fur up, "Let's have a date night." For her a date night was holding her cat like a baby and turning on *Mad Men* on her Apple TV. It was sad and she knew it. She would eventually order Chinese from the questionable place down the road and wait for someone or something to reach out to her.

Tyler finally came online.

Tyler Kiosk: I couldn't fall asleep again last night

Zoe Clark: At least you didn't have weird high school dreams like I did.

Tyler Kiosk: Legit?

Zoe Clark: Therapist doesn't seem to make much of it. Says most people have dreams of being stuck in high school. It's just a typical stress dream.

She said this even though it wasn't true. She didn't sleep either and stayed out late last night doing coke with her work friends instead. He'd judge and she just couldn't take any more of it. Even the best of friends annoy us at times.

Tyler Kiosk: Why must I always need coffee

Tyler said this so routinely to the point where it no longer meant anything.

As usual she had absolutely no response to this and changed the subject as her cat wiggled out of her arms.

Zoe Clark: What'd you end doing last night anyways?

Tyler Kiosk: Nothing. Just hung out with the buddies from work. Went to a barcade.

Zoe Clark: Fun stuff

If she was in person, she'd give a thumb up or give a fist bump, but she was far away. So, she just added a smiley emoji and left it at that.

Tyler Kiosk: It was alright. Drank cider beer and did our geek thing. Spent a while playing air hockey.

Zoe Clark: Cool. Sounds like you had a good time.

Zoe knew he didn't go to a barcade and play fun games. And they definitely were not friends of his from work. They were online people who he someone played Dungeons and Dragons together. She really didn't care about the lie and pretended to pay attention because it was easier.

Zoe loved how she and Tyler could talk about nothing while never really giving a shit about what the other person was saying. It was like some kind of fucked up therapy where they gave empathy but didn't really listen.

Zoe Clark: I haven't been feeling well

Tyler Kiosk: Yea?

Zoe Clark: Yea...I started the Lexapro a few days ago.

Tyler Kiosk: That's lit

His response threw her, and she wasn't sure if this was sincere or douchey.

Zoe Clark: Is it supposed to be making me so jittery and sick? I messaged the psych online and told her about the symptoms. She's probably gonna put me on something else next time I see her. I legit woke up the other day in a cold sweat and my mind can't focus on anything right now.

Tyler Kiosk: Ah gotchu. Yeah, I'm not sure whether SSRI's work for people like us.

Zoe resented Tyler for comparing her mental illness to his. He was completely incapable of maintaining normal friendships and work habits whereas she was capable of doing both. She might spend most of her life passively wishing she would die, but she'd be high functioning until that happened. She was so high functioning that few people even knew there was anything wrong with her.

Zoe Clark: I feel like the psych barely spoke to me before she prescribed that. How can she just know what medicine to prescribe me based on a fucking piece of paper I filled out on a clipboard? I barely understood the questions. They felt so loaded.

Tyler Kiosk: Maybe when you go back you should try asking about trying an atypical antidepressant like Trazodone.

Zoe Clark: What's that?

Tyler Kiosk: A different type of antidepressant. It won't mess with your serotonin levels as much.

Zoe Clark: how does it differ?

Tyler was well-versed in the world of medicine as a fellow fucked up person.

It took a while, but he typed back.

Tyler Kiosk: Not exactly sure overall how to explain it. It acts differently than SSRIs. Basically, from what I understand that instead of blocking the reuptake of serotonin, it enhances production instead...

He definitely was using that extra time to look that shit up online.

Zoe Clark: Hmm might be a good one. I'll see what the doctor suggests. I just feel bad like I couldn't tough it out long enough or something. Like I'm pathetic for not being able to handle such a low dose of Zoloft.

Tyler Kiosk: Not true at all. You are not pathetic.

Zoe Clark: Feel pathetic. I shouldn't have said anything. I should have just waited till the appointment and stuck it out.

Tyler Kiosk: You tried and what is important is that you find something that causes the least amount of side effects while effectively treating your condition.

Zoe Clark: I suppose. I'm scared to try anything new now. I didn't know I could react that way to a drug and this whole process is putting me off.

Tyler Kiosk: This one med wasn't it. So try another. Something will work.

Zoe Clark: I guess.

Zoe didn't really know what else to say at this point, and they spent the next several minutes typing but not sending. It seemed like forever.

Tyler Kiosk: Okay ... So fresh rain and fresh cut grass do not have a good smell together. Each alone are great but together just smell like wet dog.

They'd spoken for so many months that Tyler had a cool way of knowing when Zoe was done being heavy. No one could be heavy for too long. It wouldn't be good, and he hated when things weren't good although this rarely happened between them.

Zoe Clark: Ewww. That doesn't sound a good smell at all.

Tyler Kiosk: No. It's aweful.

Zoe Clark: Awe-ful?

Tyler Kiosk: YES...I was full of awe.

As the night dragged on and the messages kept coming, all she could think about was whether it was time to go back home. When she was at work, she was in what felt like a fugue state but here she was smiling. Was the job the problem or the city? Zoe mused to Minion on possible alternative jobs she could take in San Francisco waitress, truck driver, movie projector projectionist, In and Out Burger employee, Uber driver...

There really were no good options left for her there. She couldn't tell him. She couldn't feel like a failure who wanted to pivot again.

The Adventures of Zoe and the Hipster Named Desya

Everything was fine and then it wasn't. She was the same as everyone else and forgot that. She didn't know why she thought her experiences would be unique. It was all so typical...

Desya's backyard was bigger than his whole apartment complex put together. His girlfriend, Sonya, was designing a Zen garden back there. Zoe wondered if the landlord allowed that or if he just didn't know. She went to Brooklyn with some friends a few years back in the middle of a snowstorm to see her friend Isaac and the people she stayed with had a similar setup. Their deal was that their landlord never came around, so they never checked to see what was cool and what wasn't. As long as they kept the landlord's Mother Theresa statue in the back, they vibed that they'd be fine.

She couldn't imagine things in Brooklyn were much different these days.

But Zoe was now in Berkley, California with Desya. He was a friend of a friend back in Chicago. She thought they were relatively close to campus but couldn't be sure. Zoe really needed to start paying attention more. She had felt the walls around her back in her Oakland apartment closing in and needed to just get out so Desya let her have his couch for the night. It wasn't permanent fix, but it was like drowning and coming for air. Temporary relief.

That night they got together with other friends to listen to folk music at Café Med. Seemed like everyone she knew there was either originally from Chicago like her or a friend of theirs. Desya and Zoe sauntered off to get some greasy goodness and she asked him if he ever "considered people."

He said, "sometimes."

She stared at the workers hustling to prepare orders and wipe their faces with greasy hands. She asked him if they were to consider us right now, what would we notice. He paused in his stoic mischievousness and pointed out that the workers were trapped.

It was vague and off-putting. Yet Zoe understood. Desya was always good at making complex ideas simple. She believed it came from the fact that he had to grow up in a two-language home. When you are forced to translate back and forth you learn to speak tersely.

"I have never worked a 12-hour shift on no sleep. I never have worked a menial labor job. My father was forced to work at a young age after his father walked out. He always told me that he didn't have an adolescence so I shouldn't burden mine with too much responsibility. He wonders why I'm so entitled. I don't think I could bring myself to work a job like this anyhow. It wasn't too much responsibility. I'm just too far ahead in life to do something as childish as scrapping fat vats and serving fries," he went off.

The woman behind the counter finally rang up their order: two burgers and a side of fries.

Zoe got a cup for water and filled it with Mountain Dew. She was clearly depraved. She asked Desya why he thought they made the water cups clear and small. He said it was obviously so that they could see who was stealing soda.

He added that said Mountain Dew would have probably only cost the company 10 cents. Her sense of depravity and remorse was lifted as she placed four pennies and a dime on the drip tray.

She seemed to know her place. This wasn't it.

Desya's apartment had a painting of Che Guevara being doused with gasoline and a Coke in the forefront that reads "Fuckit". Zoe preferred Pepsi, but I guess in this situation that really doesn't matter.

She lost her mind many times.

It always came back to her in some form or another.

Zoe later on sat on the floor of his shower with her eyes closed, listening to the water hit the backs of her ears, feeling it trickle through her eyelashes, for hours and felt like this was the best she could do right now.

She woke up in the morning and couldn't bear it. But the day kept coming. Zoe sat on his porch in Berkley, California. A city that Desya's girlfriend informed her was the most liberal city in America. She asked Sonya why and she said, "Well, for one, People's Park."

She didn't give another example and looked more fucked up than Zoe did.

San Francisco was the kind of place that people like Zoe went. People who knew in their souls that they didn't belong where they came from. She was drawn to the place where the writers she was reading and the artists she was looking at had lived or passed through. But Zoe slowly realized that the people there were all alike. They were running away. In search of not something but nothing. Hoping to be more than they were. More than they are. More than anybody.

She wanted to think that if there was indeed still a world here in a hundred years that it would be because of music and poetry that it survived. That was the only thing that could save us.

She thought back to Desya on that porch and she realized he was one of them. Brave and troubled middle-class boy adrift in the night wanting to escape suburbia and the conformity of the Midwest. She never truly knew him before she migrated West to San Francisco with similar ideas except from her few interactions with him at a local Denny's in Lincolnwood, Illinois. He would show up to the diner with a canteen, and mole skinned poetry anthologies in hopes of finding validation. Or seeming interesting at least.

He was just another poor little rich boy desperately wanting to be different yet ran away to a place where everyone was the same. When he left for the West, it was a bay lit up like a Christmas tree with scruffy adolescents with dog-eared volumes of Vonnegut and Rousseau. He hung about in coffee shops that never closed and colleges that never slept until he found himself a job there.

He sat there and waited to be seen for the literary genius he felt he was. The kind that belonged alongside similar thinkers at that university. A craver of a coming literary revolution and the end of hypocrisy but it never came. So instead, he grew into another middle-aged stoner who played bongos during the weekends and put on a suit to teach MFA students during the week. The conformity never ended no matter how far he ran, and the cliché slow dripped like the espresso he drank every morning because "he just didn't feel like a human being without it".

A more enlightened mind indeed, she scoffed in her mind. There was no end to his adolescence. Just a 30-year-old boy nipping at the heels of greater men. Desya was hoping to one day rank himself amongst heroes. But there were no heroes left here and the ones he worshipped never really stayed. Just drifters who romanticized a place turned corporate. If he wanted to be different, if he genuinely wanted to be "free" like he badgered Zoe at Café Med about last night, he would've never left Chicago for a place full of the same stomping "men" like him. He would've stayed and made change there.

He came out with tea and sat there with her and Sonya. Zoe told him her thoughts, hoping for acknowledgment but was stunted by rejection. As she sat on the porch in her sadness looking for answers she already knew, she saw the boys in him desperately trying to be ingenious or cynical or ironic. Never open. Never free. Never aware of the fact that it wasn't the location that changed the person, it was the aspiration of something better, regardless of where it may be.

Don't Quit Your Daydream

The March air was warm, and bursts of light spilled between the front two driver seats of the van as she drove with the three guys who she found going her way. Two were guys from Cornell going back from Spring break and the other from Iowa. I-80 was a natural route for them to take and she'd taken the exact same road two years earlier, just the other way around.

The sun felt like an old movie theatre projector hitting through the windshield. In movies they call this golden hour. Her and Desya's mutual friend back in Chicago told her this. Now she couldn't get it out of her mind. Then a stop motion scene scattered across the pavement like apparitions on the highway driving 89 miles per hour through the dessert heading into the night.

The dying light was just enough to keep Zoe, curled up in the back like a fetus, aware. That night was like her first night on earth and she was being reborn. Almost 30 years of walking and living, but only then did she really start to open her eyes and dared to do something different than what had been planned for her or even what she had planned for herself. She was without regrets though and looking down at the black pavement from her car window she felt a weight lift off her with each place they passed that she recognized from her trip two years before.

Zoe was a sheltered girl from the Chicago northwest suburbs, hundreds of miles from home, packed into a strange red minivan with no heat or AC with three guys she had only met the night before, all dressed for different climates. She naively remained in her clothes from San Francisco, forgetting the bipolar weather that she was headed toward. As the sun died and the stars rose, cool air crept into the car from all angles. Thankfully, it was packed with backpacks, boxes, random clothes, and three other warm bodies scattered about. There would be no odd On the Road experience where they would be dying for warmth and look for it in places better left untouched.

She slushed her toes between one of her backpacks and a box full of cassette tapes. It was an old van and that's the only format of music it could play. The fact that any of them still had cassettes was wild. Hers were back at her parent's house with cool art made from colored pencils and names on the label on front. She felt proud of her mixtapes and the names she gave them. Things like: "My life is a movie," "I'm at an all-time low," "Hype, "or "I'm ashamed of this playlist." Instead, she was stuck there listening to Metallica.

She wasn't sure whether there were frats at Cornell or not, but the songs on were the definition of Frat Boy Rock. She half expected Flo Rida or Beastie Boys to pop on next. A name for that tape could've been "It's All Greek to Them" but without knowing whether they were frat boys or not, she decided to keep that suggestion to herself. She also didn't want to embarrass them. It's not as if the music was ridiculously bad or anything. She had just aged out of it.

Music is almost like politics and religion. People get weirdly defensive over it and who was she to talk? When she was their age she was listening to College Rock like The Smiths and Hüsker Dü. The more depressed, the better.

She shifted around and pooled her weight upon Radley's shoulder and the window next to her since there was nowhere else to go. He was the guy headed to Iowa and he didn't mind. He barely spoke and she found this fascinating about him. They huddled in for what would be a 12-hour dash or more to get through the night and beat the tedium of the Cornhusker state. Nebraska for those who are unaware. Zoe called it the bumfuck state and instantly regretted it once when referring to it like that at a party when she was talking to someone she didn't know was a Nebraskan. Dude got defensive and left.

Have I mentioned yet that some people are sensitive about weird things? Perhaps we can add home states to the list of things not to talk about with strangers like politics, religion, and music.

As someone from Illinois she had no issues when people made fun of it, but that was just Zoe's personality. She knew she came from the middle of nowhere and that her city was a Democratic oasis surrounded by farmland. That it was a haven of political corruption and the only real culture people thought it had was its food.

Back to Nebraska though, everyone in that car was determined to speed through it as fast as possible. One would get motion sickness from looking out the window while driving in that state. Just nothing for miles on both sides. The government itself knew how mundane Nebraska was and artificially made gentle grades and engineered curves to deter car accidents from tired drivers losing their sense of object permanence while passing through.

As the early morning sky rose like a curtain on horizon, the once cold window warmed the back of her neck that rested on it. She looked out the window and it hit her in the gut. They hadn't made it through Nebraska yet. The state before her eyes, not much different from the one she'd fallen asleep to, was shining now at least and it was warm enough where she might be able to take a break and get out of the van. Change was still ahead of her but she had little to pass the time. The windows were covered with dust, so she gazed down at road below her to pass the time. The earth ¬was just a succession of sad dirt, craters, and potholes that would probably never be fixed. They were there two years ago so there was little evidence that gave her hope that anyone intended to do anything at all.

Zoe searched at her feet for a paper product of any kind to write on and came across an unused Subway napkin. Dudes were gross.

"There is a whole wide world out there", she scribbled, "A world hidden to only those who have enough hunger to seek it and enough energy to fix it."

Her stomach unsettled as she wrote the word: hunger.

Driving 15 miles on a dry run, the needle of the gas gauge flickered on empty like a broken amplifier. Radley was still asleep next to her in the back like a sweet, nestled baby boy unfettered by the kicks and hustles of the new day. The Cornell boys in front tweaked and howled like cattle hands in a slap-happy attempt to jeer the van to their mark:

"Oi! We haven't made it yet, old girl! GO GO GO," Macky, shirtless on the passenger side, his jowls stuffed with chewing tobacco from a tin can, slapped the red minivan's side cajoling. She cringed at the awkwardness of it and was weirdly reminded of her older brother's college roommate from Kentucky. She had to play DD for the two once and dude legit spit out chewing tobacco from her car. It was just the height of hickness...if there even is such a word, but that's a story for another time.

"This carcass ain't seen the darkest yet! We still have mountains and 1200 miles to go! SO GO!" Macky could just not shut up. He was more awake than everyone in the car combined and she couldn't decide if he was just insane or had too much coffee.

The two Cornell guys looked back at her laughing with each other like they knew an inside joke, and Zoe nodded sheepishly, disheveled from the long night. She slowly noticed Radley stir awake and felt a bit more relaxed now that she was not the only person not in on whatever the hell it was that the other two were in on.

Radley muttered, "Who in the fuck was just shouting and why?" and Zoe just laughed with her eyes fixed on Macky.

"Who do you think," she faintly said to Radley and he smiled with amusement.

"Figures," he slowly rubbed the tiredness out of his eyes and smiled like a kid that had just woken up from an afternoon nap.

She couldn't decide if she was more excited that she wasn't the only one who thought Macky was crazy or if it was the fact that Radley was speaking to her. She laughed and sighed, "Dear god, I can't believe I got into a car with such morons..."

"They aren't morons, Zo" he said. "They're rich boys and they're just doing what rich boys do. Get loud and have weird main character moments."

She immediately remembered back in school when she went on a few dates with a trust funder. He shaved his head, smoked opium, and even jumped into Lake Michigan in October. People with money will do just about anything to seem interesting.

She was so caught up in remembering that she even dated that idiot that she barely noticed Radley was still quietly talking to her, "I've seen it for years. You'd think you'd have witnessed it more too. You look like you're more my age than theirs. The minute they get a chance, they haul themselves into cars with backpacks, bandanas, and granola bars hoping that they instantly will become characters out of a Kerouac novel. If that's something either of those two are on the inside, who knows? It feels fake though."

He pointed at Macky's backpack at their feet that had a copy of the book, Into The Wild sticking out. She never read it but saw the movie. Immediately, she remembered the quote: "It's important in life not necessarily to be strong but to feel strong. To measure yourself at least once. To find yourself at least once in the most ancient of human conditions. Facing the blind death stone alone, with nothing to help you but your hands and your own head."

Was this Macky? She pondered this for a while and then started to have a mini existential crisis. Why had she never felt the need to go to extreme lengths to LIVE and holler out of car windows like she'd never seen the sun before?

Radley saw Zoe's eyes grow distant and knew she had to be reassured.

"You aren't a character because you don't have the luxury to be. You are Zoe Clark and you're just an actual fucking human being. Some people feel like that they need validation and at least one great moment in life that defines them. Macky won't ever do this again. He's gonna go back to school and become a lawyer and talk about shit like this for years. I'm not even sure he's doing it now to be happy or just acting the way he thinks he needs to have a cool moment for when he tells this story to his friends later. But you, you're real. Quiet, yes. But you recognize that life is more than a story that someone can tell in a bar. You're worried that you aren't present and the only reason that you're heading home is that you're trying to close the gaps of your past. But I vibed you feeling joy earlier. When the sun hit your neck. When you looked at the tapes. You were here. You just didn't go wild and shout your excitement out of a window like some crazy jackass on a 5-hour energy kick."

She immediately realized that Radley wasn't quiet because he was shy. He was quiet because he was just taking everything in. Even her and the stupid things she scribbled on napkins while they drove through the night. This both weirded her out and gave her comfort.

The minivan hmmphd and sighed as they finally pulled into a gas station. Radley shifted around in the backseat in order for Zoe to get out while he hung back.

"Okay, I'm gonna fill up. Let's all take a bit to stretch our legs, go to the bathroom, and be back in five," the other Cornell guy said as he fished around for gas money in the cup holder where they all pooled their money the day before.

Zoe took in a breath of fresh air, "I'm gonna grab an Arnold Palmer, I'll pay the clerk."

The other Cornell guy handed her the wrinkled-up money and she headed in, her knees swelling from disuse.

Zoe lingered in the store, waking herself up by wandering aisles. She shuffled aimlessly between shelves of Pop-Tarts and candy bars, considering whether she should buy a snack as well, but she didn't have enough cash. So she just settled on getting the $1 drink she originally came in for.

Back in the freezer section between soda and beer were the Arnold Palmers and another intriguing drink called Peace Tea. She noted this as something to try later when she had more cash. Glancing back at the man behind the counter as she grabbed her drink and headed towards him. He was sad and unshaven. Not like the 7-Eleven guys back home. They were always energetic and happy to greet her in the morning. This happened even when she wasn't a regular. She assumed that this was either due to company policy or if people in Nebraska were just as sad as she was to be in the state.

That man had to have worked there at the KwikShop for at least 10 years but for him it had to have been forever. A necktie hung down from beneath his shirt tucked under his uniform, like every day he was prepared for the unlikely event that things would get better and that he would move up in this world into a position that would actually require a necktie at work. Perhaps that was the difference. This was a white guy in Nebraska and probably thought he could do anything he could set his mind to, like we were taught in school. He looked like the very definition of white privilege gone wrong. Not to stereotype, but the guys back home were all immigrants, and they were more than excited to have their own business and just be alive. It clearly wasn't enough for this guy. The day was dead, the new sun still new, and she could tell he was already bored, patiently waiting for a rush that wouldn't come. She was his only costumer, dawdling around in his store with no direction hoping to prepare her skinny legs for the next bout of driving for which she would be taking the wheel.

Eventually, Zoe grew tired of the dawdling. The dudes in the car outside were getting impatient so she paid the man for the gas and her drink and smiled. When the world beats you down and sucks out all the life, only a something as genuine and real as a smile stands the chance of making things better. He smiled back and told her, "it's on the house." He then suggested she grab one of the snacks she was eyeing before and then in his infinite boredom decided to draw.

Zoe lingered, knowing damn well that he didn't need to be that chill. She just grabbed a candy bar from beneath counter and hung with him for a bit. The dudes outside could wait.

"This is gonna be a self-portrait," he announced to her like a magician, as if almost to say, "for my next trick I really really need to feel validated." She was happy to oblige.

He rummaged in his backpack below the counter as she lifted the tab to open her drink; he looked up and smirked as it popped open. Holding up a coffee-stained legal pad and pen he had found in the bag successfully, he flipped passed the next week's schedule, the order and shipping information, and notes that almost looked like blackout poems, to a blank page and positioned himself to get to work.

"You know what? I'm gonna make this for both of us. Self-portraits are boring and right now, I'm not by myself. This is going to be us as if we were stars in the sky", he smirked, "here I will draw a constellation and a comet and dark matter and all of it will be me."

Dark matter is composed of particles that do not absorb, reflect, or emit light. She immediately became intrigued as hell as to how someone might draw dark matter.

He tore the paper from the pad, laying it out next to register, the pad and its bothersome responsibilities now tossed aside and out of sight.

"And next, I will draw the sun, new and shining. That will be you," he gestured toward her. Zoe sipped on her Arnold Palmer dutifully leaning in watching his fingers manipulate the pen up and down the sheet of yellow paper. She'd watched the TV show Cosmos several times and was determined this dude either had no idea what he was talking about or was an absolute genius.

The strangeness of all of it was not lost on her. She had set out two years ago to witness something strange and new and here it was at a Nebraska gas station.

Life is weird as hell sometimes and we never truly understand why things end up the way they do until we die. She instantly thought of a Steve Jobs speech where he spoke about connecting the dots in life and that you can't do it looking forward. That you just need to trust that they will connect somehow. Zoe wondered if this was one of her dots.

Gas station guy flipped the now star-clad paper horizontally and began labeling planets, moons, and stars. One star was named "procrastination", another "regret". She immediately began to understand where his mind was going.

He had planets orbiting her sun that was labeled "kind stranger" and in the nothingness that he explained to her was dark matter, he wrote in big showy capital letters, "MORE". She leaned on the counter from her elbows to her wrists watching him like a TV at midnight. Like her mind had just been expanded but her body was not yet aware of it. He had the air of a pitchman, the way he danced and showboated behind the counter, gallantly selling Zoe his ideas with his art. This is how she imagined Buddhist monks taught their students in the mountains of Tibet, but here there were no monks or mountains. Instead, she was standing at a Kwik- Stop in Nebraska in torn leggings and oversized t-shirt. But teaching was done nonetheless.

A customer soon walked in, wearing a bomber jacket and tie. As the door swung open the clerk quickly shuffled the papers out of site so not to arouse prying eyes. They exchanged looks as they watched this third wheel enter like an outsider.

The man, who looked to be a travelling salesman, fumbled around like she had before. He was the kind of guy that lived out of rest stops likes this, sauntering around and biding his time before he would have to go into his next account or the local motel. She knew the life. Her father spent most of his career doing just that. The salesman grabbed a cheap pumpkin spiced latte made from powder and headed to the counter to be rung up.

He left, disappointed with the lack of conversation and visibly bothered by Zoe and the clerk's strange stares. The clerk took his sketch of the universe back out and stared at it for a while, confident and unbothered by Zoe's presence.

He smiled and began making constellations from the stars.

Soon the paper was a mess of lines connecting the "procrastination" with the "regret" amongst other things. There were still asteroids passing through and the planets were left unbothered. But in the middle of the lines that began to take the shape of a man made of stars were the giant letters "MORE" sprawled out across the chest. And the man looked at her and stared.

Zoe leaned forward and gestured to the shape of the man on the paper and said, "Ambivalent."

Embarrassed, his heavy head in his tired, damp hands, "Sorry?"

"Ambivalent. The man looks ambivalent; I can't tell which way he's going or if he's even going at all."

"You're right. Do you know what it feels like to feel two entirely opposite ways at the exact same time?" She thought for a hot minute, and then said," I think that's the difference between 'being' and 'becoming." She looked out the window to see Macky and the other dude in the back seat of the car and Radley coming to get her.

She immediately said, "I've gotta pee," when Radley came through the door and ducked out to the bathroom. She needed a second to be alone with all those thoughts going on in her mind and, also, she drank that Arnold Palmer fast. Really fast.

When she went to wash her hands after, she couldn't get these thoughts out of her head. She hated the façade that she had become. She inspected further. She felt confused but wasn't exactly sure. When did this start, she wondered? After John died? When Tyler kept pushing for her to come home? How long was living this way? Just skirting around this earth, priming other people to consider her "lost". Absent even....

Zoe stepped to the sink next to a girl attached to big wet boots. Her mother was probably the person in the far stall still. There were no mirrors in this place, which was odd as fuck, but this didn't stop Zoe from watching herself like there was one. She sought reflection and validation on any and everything that gives it. The guy at the register really got in her head. The way Tyler did sometimes.

This is why depressed people shouldn't mingle. It warps into something too big for either to handle and someone always ends up in a bathroom somewhere crying until Xanax kicks in.

I know this from experience and Zoe did too.

It seemed vain to get such relief from your own face, Zoe thought while standing at that bathroom sink, staring at a blank wall. She began to swig the mouthwash she brought from the car. It tasted like cancer, and mid-gargle she got the urge to vomit, but she didn't. The woman at the sink to her left was judging. As a society we've designated this breed of human as Karens and this one was not amused or pleased to be sharing space with a person like Zoe.

A line formed behind Zoe and her sink. At least two people were waiting for her to finish. Whatever they thought she was doing they seem to be under the impression she should be about done by now. But Zoe could stand there all day. She was that person in the gas station bathroom doing something she shouldn't be doing. She really knew better. She was being selfish. She was making them wait. She was making Radley stand awkwardly in the store while Macky was probably impatiently waiting back in the car high off of life or hopefully sleeping by now. But she came in here for a reason.

She had to pee. Done.

She had to fix her hair. Done.

She had to brush her teeth. She did mouthwash instead. She barely swished the first bit so she decided to try again.

The Karen behind her gave up judging her and just left. She made an audible gawf and used hand sanitizer from her purse instead. Zoe deserved that gawf. She was holding up the line. But the paper towel dispenser over the sink kept showing her reflection and she couldn't stop looking. It's like she kept resetting. Not just there. But in everything. It would seem that she was perpetually at the beginning. This dim adolescent, would-be adult, was constantly reincarnating, reliving the same mistakes, day by day with different sources so that she might someday reach clarity. She hated this cycle and wanted out. She needed escape. She spit her mouthwash out in a disgusting way and hoped that the Karen saw that before she had left. Zoe turned her gaze to the left hoping to make eye contact with someone. But as her eyes searched, they met not a pair of stomping heels or converse, but big wet boots and the little girl that belonged to them.

"Are you homeless", she skeptically asked Zoe whilst twiddling on some smart phone that wasn't from Apple.

Zoe's mouth hung open as her eyes met the girl's and wanted to immediately correct her.

"Of course I'm not homeless," Zoe wanted to say.

"Do you know any homeless people with an iPhone?" Zoe would have challenged.

"I'm wearing hundred-dollar shoes," she would've pointed out.

But Zoe said nothing. She was ushered out by Radley's voice telling her to hurry up.

After she returned from the bathroom and apologized to Radley for taking so long, she saw it taped to the register, the back of the picture the cash register guy made with the words in all caps," FUCK IT I QUIT." She imagined he felt relief and was no longer ambivalent after their weird interaction. Radley merely told her that the guy left with his tie in hand and the two of them hopped back into the van to continue driving.

It's a Mood

A sudden jolt of motion woke Zoe. She was in a shitty van outside of her parent's house. She grew up there outside of Chicago but not far away enough from the city where she couldn't just say "I'm from Chicago," when people asked. Like most major cities, people don't really care what the names of the surrounding suburbs are. They just want to know what the nearest name-worthy place is.

When a person is lucky enough to grow up in a state with a major city, the answer is always easy. Especially if you're a Democrat and don't wish to be associated with any rural area that might close. Chicago was one of those annoying cities. A booming metropolis that was surrounded by farmland on almost ends except to the East which hugged Lake Michigan. Without the lake though, it would be straddling the border of Indiana making it completely surrounded by rednecks. But that doesn't mean the city wasn't huge. It was once called the "Second City" by others until LA happened, but Chicago never stopped calling itself that. Just like how the Sears Tower changed its name to something no one bothered to learn, because it would always just be the Sears Tower. Chicagoans be like that.

Zoe grabbed her things from the van and headed in to her parent's home. Like most Millennials, she knew she was going to have to stay there for a bit until she figured out where to go next in life. She knew the general locations she would be going: the city. But she had no idea what neighborhood she'd live in or how to make money to pay her rent when she did finally leave.

It wasn't until later that night when Zoe truly realized that she really was no longer in the car, making her way home from San Francisco. Perhaps she never was. Maybe she had been stuck in a fugue state this entire time; a dream maybe that she concocted while doing too many drugs or in a manic episode. Something about being back in her parent's house did that to her. She was never truly happy at home even though she lied and told people she grew up in just a normal family. The true story was that she knew she wanted to leave that place when she was twelve years old. She began concocting her plan to leave by seventeen. She finally got out at nineteen and never went back. She only returned to get a taste of the environment during short visits and holiday gatherings. Even during those she realized that the place never felt right, and her family always kept her on edge. She'd developed an anxiety disorder at seventeen, due to the stress they put on her. Perhaps that's why it was at that age she started concocting the plan.

As narrator, I'm here to state that Zoe did not grow up in an abusive home. Just a busy one where she was largely ignored and when she wasn't being ignored she was being lectured about not being good enough.

Zoe began to sink into a saddening feeling. A mean case of the reds. Her heart pounded and it was only then that she realized that she had no medication on her to help her ride out what felt like a panic attack.

She grabbed her headphones and began listening to Tom Waits in hopes that a distraction would prevent an oncoming episode where she felt like she was going to die. Instead, it made her feel like she was a passenger on train hurdling forward on a fixed track. This wasn't something she'd felt in almost a decade. She was racing forward in her mind, not knowing where she was going or why, but there was an endless black abyss ahead.

Years ago, a therapist told Zoe if she ever felt such panic that she should attempt visualization exercises, so she decided to stick with the train thing and somehow find a way off it. She imagined walking through in the train and not paying attention to the speed or direction that it was going. Instead, she would go searching for where peculiar music was coming from. It was the Tom Waits music, but she knew that if she didn't keep it within the realms of the train she'd slip out of the exercise. So she had "Old Shoes" on repeat and let that lead her to the dining car of the train only to find that the only other person on the train was him. A drunken balladeer who had fewer answers than she did. The only thing he bothered to tell her when he wasn't strumming his guitar in a surrealist manner was that nobody was driving the train. They were the only people on it. No conductors, passengers, or even a radio to call for help. The veracity of what he said hit her like water and she came to the deep, visceral conclusion that she was the only person who could stop it. He had no stakes in this and actually seemed to enjoy the idea of going nowhere. Zoe searched all cars of the train looking for breaks even though she had no idea what they would look like if she found them.

But then there was a loud screech, and the train stopped. For some reason though, she was still on it. She thought for a moment and then considered that maybe the speed and fixed rail wasn't the problem at all. Maybe it was something on the train. Even thought there were no passengers, there was luggage everywhere. MacBooks, ideas, phones, principles, beliefs and nostalgia.

As a kid, Zoe would ask for a toy train set every Christmas. She never got it. This hurt her for a long time and then hurt her even more when she confronted her parents about it when she was an adult. Yes, they knew she wanted it. Yes, they could afford it. No, they would not get it for her. It was a toy for boys. It was a knife in her heart.

As she worked her way through her visualization exercise she finally came to the conclusion that since she and Tom Waits were the only people on the train this luggage belonged to them. Or maybe just her. She began trying to think of anything the Headspace guy would say at this moment, but the only thing she really remembered from that app was taking deep breaths and Blue Sky Awareness. Without the app on her phone she couldn't recall the exact words but in her mind all she could concoct was this: "Imagine a sky filled with gray clouds, now look beyond them. Remind yourself of the fact that those all clouds are passing and dissipate over time. Sometimes they are white and complimentary and other times all you can see is darkness and intricacies of gray. Now take away the clouds and look towards the bigger picture. The blue sky behind the clouds, behind the gray. The blue sky is how it really is. The clouds are just your feelings. Your clouds will pass."

In an effort to make her anxiety go away and make the two exercises work she attempted to replace the word clouds with luggage. She couldn't decide if they were meant to just be fleeting things and she should leave them be or dig deeper. The harshness of the screeching and stress she felt when it came to luggage made the whole thing bothersome, so she decided that she no longer wanted to be on the train. Zoe especially needed to get off before it started moving forward again into the abyss. She couldn't be sure of how long she had so she jumped.

As she did some of the cargo went with her, bothering her more. Part of her wished she had never visualized the train or the clouds or any of it in the first place. Perhaps she should've just allowed the panic attack to happen and be done with it all by now. The only thing she knew at that moment though was that she had to thrust forward. Since the luggage came off with her as she jumped off the train, she decided that it wanted her to go through it. As Zoe rummaged through the bags, the rush of it all lessened; looking through things and saying to herself, "Fuck, I never I needed this..." "Why is this thing here?" "Damn, this is one isn't even mine!" The weight of it all lightens and with it comes an autonomy that Zoe never felt before that night, and before she knew it, her eyes opened, and she was back at home.

Within her was an actively cognizant person capable of kindness, malice, altruism, patience, edginess, openness, selfishness, and absolute empathy. Through her luggage she was able to pour out all of that along with her old belongings and nostalgic feelings. Some beautiful. Others painful. Her mind did become clouded for a mere second but then remembered the blue.

It was nice to be home, but she needed to find her people and where she wanted to go in life.

Kurt Shirt

She hung around the house in a sweaty Kurt Cobain T-shirt that she got from her ex-boyfriend when she was 18. She stole it. He didn't give it to her. Or really she just never gave it back. Relationships are weird that way. She liked to wear his things when they dated, finding random excuses to throw on his hoodies or shirts, like the cold or the rain or that she fell into a fuck ton of mud while they were hiking and needed to change. They broke up on a sunny day in April over the phone. He made fun of Catholics and she was born one, even though she didn't believe in it. She was bothered because she considered his weird Christian church cultish. When they spoke on the phone, she wasn't sure if she meant to, or if she really just wanted him to fight her on it. She liked to fight, and he didn't. So that call was doomed to fail. Three days later he came to her house at night with Stevie Nicks CDs and books hoping to bribe her for affection and fix the relationship, but it was too little too late, and she had moved on. Things were easy like that at 20. Weeks later she would go through her things, picking up the clothes off her floor like her mother demanded, and find his old T-shirt with the prodigal son of grunge on the front smoking his cigarette, his stringy greasy hair distended from all sides, stoic and not caring.

She shoved it in with the rest of her clothes and decided that that's the collateral damage of a relationship, the price her ex would pay for not fighting. And she would smile every time a new boyfriend or girlfriend would wear it, marking the shirt with their scent and leaving stains all over it something that was once his.

As Zoe hung around thinking this, she decided that she should probably go and give him his shirt back, if he even remembered. She heard
that he worked at a bookstore in Wicker Park. She decided to go there
tomorrow and then go to Wormhole, her favorite coffee shop, and write
for the rest of the day.

For that exact moment, however, she had to clean her bedroom. Her
mother wasn't about to do that shit for her anymore.

Madly, Truly, Deeply

Where does a life begin? Does anything ever really start when we say it did? Are the stories we post online just made up of trivial clichés, staged photos, and scraps of optimism?

These are things that Zoe Clark thought of that day when she was looking at Craigslist for roommates and jobs. She hit up the friends who begged her to come back but they had nothing except invitations to get coffee sometime soon.

Her mother came home with McDonald's and asked how the "job hunt" was going as she sat down and looked over Zoe's shoulder, a habit that Zoe was used to back in high school but was now something that made her apprehensive. There was just a constant nagging feeling in the back of her mind that if her mom saw her failing, she would never feel loved again.

So she closed her MacBook and ate burgers at the counter for a while with her mom. It was one of the things she missed and was now taking for granted. Her mind was elsewhere, and she was just dutifully nodding every time her mom said something.

Her parents had plans for her over a decade ago but now she was lost and didn't know what to do next. Zoe Clark's biggest fear was complacency and that somewhere along the way she might forget that she picked this path for herself and rebelled against her parent's plans for her. She skirmished for it and slowly made it out of that house and became who she thought she wanted to be. But now she was back eating burgers at the counter with her mom just like she used to do in high school.

There was this overwhelming feeling of shame. She didn't believe in god or any maker but if there was one, they gave her an insurmountable amount of ambition. She was wasting it. Her father used to lecture her all the time about how much potential she had but she could never seem to live up to it. Whichever path she had taken so far ended in sadness and setbacks. She saw depression where there once was ambition. She saw shame where there should have been happiness, and then she saw a message from Tyler on her phone asking if he wanted to check out a new bar downtown.

Maybe They Will Have Tacos:
A Goal, an Aspiration

Something insane had happened in Zoe's experience of temporality. Time had like tripled in speed since a week and a half ago. It was insane. It used to be painful to wait for it to pass while she was at work and now it was just instantly over. She wondered if it was somehow linked to a change in her serotonin levels since forgetting her meds in San Francisco. She felt like her psychiatrist secretly hated her. That they maybe saw her as a narcissist or sociopath or bitch or whatever, so she stopped taking them unless she really felt the need to.

She came out as a poet to her friend Tyler the other night at a bar in Logan Square. Zoe couldn't remember the name because they had been to so many. This one had games in it so she thought it was more of a "barcade" than a bar. It was about time that she told Tyler though because he was really starting to question her sanity when she said weeks earlier that she might fly back home instead of driving and that she should take weed back on the plane and call it performance art.

Zoe told Tyler it was a joke but she didn't tell him that she brought the weed back home anyways. Not by plane or by car, but by mail. Loopholes. He didn't have to know. He didn't have to judge. He just needed to enjoy that drink with her and pretend that two years apart didn't change either of them.

For inquiring minds: she didn't just mail marijuana to herself. That felt like something only rookies would do. She shipped it back home to her parent's house under a fake return address. She then tucked it in a random t-shirt that she bought at a bar a year earlier but never wore and threw it in a package. She almost felt like the Unabomber for a split second.

After her drink with Tyler, she decided that she would light up and then grab some tacos down the road. Logan Square was a great neighborhood to score tacos.

The weed fucked her up instead. Or maybe it was the shift in her temporality. Either way, she started to hallucinate so immediately went back home in an Uber.

When she got back home, she threw herself in bed and hoped it would end soon. During her hallucination, the fan in her bedroom started moving. The light fixtures started rotating, the entire fan became a bio-organic substance, and it morphed into a variety of faces. Sometimes it would flash, and a black and white face would overtake the entire fan. Other times, it seemed that the fan was alive, and the center of the fan was a face chewing on an arm.

She kept getting up from her bed and walking into the kitchen or into the bathroom to stare into the mirror. Everything else appeared normal. At first the fan only moved around when her glasses were off. When she put them on it looked like a normal fan. But then one time she put her glasses on and it was still in its surreal form and the screws on the fan started moving around all over the fan. After a while shadowy sigils descended from the fan and entered her chest. Zoe was like 'I'm going to die in here and everyone will think I just died of dehydration or something.' She decided to leave. But then she decided 'no I'll stay I probably shouldn't wander.' Then she went back and lay down on her bed and dagger-like appendages slowly extended out from the center of the fan toward her chest and she was like 'ok now I'm leaving'.

She was thirty, and she should've been able to handle it herself but, for some reason, she decided to walk to her sister's house. One time when she was seventeen, she got too high with the dealer down the street and went to her sister's house for help. She legit only lived maybe a ten-minute walk away. Her name was Kelsey. She chilled Zoe out and the next day pretended that it never happened. To this day, Zoe didn't know if it was weed that fucked her up or something called "spice". She told Kelsey that she was just having a panic attack at the time, and Kelsey just went with it. The day after she didn't say anything about it, but Zoe knew that Kelsey understood it wasn't just a panic attack.

When she got to Kelsey's, she let herself in and vomited into the sink. Things like the text on newspapers and magazines were moving around and the iPhone on their table looked like it was undulating. Kelsey heard Zoe come in and immediately assumed "drunk" and tried to get a bit of liquid in her before sending her upstairs to go to sleep. As Zoe sat down in the bed in the dark a sigil came out of her chest, glowing orange, and there were shadowy figures on the walls and ceiling, one of them was glowing blue and yellow.

Suddenly she felt extremely calm and immediately fell asleep. The next day she felt completely normal and finally got tacos. Kelsey said nothing.

Zoe Clark's #SquadGoals:

1) I will come to you from the woods of the suburb surrounded by highways adolescent. We will start a rave with all our friends, instagram it and get all the likes.

2) I am bittersweet and poetry tweeting. A sad merrymaker on a cliff. There is a Happy hipster girl beside me leaning off the edge planted in a digital blandness with a cat. A desert of ello and goodbyes, and books made of faces she never knew. She takes a selfie midjump and I wave goodbye, cat in hand.

3) I wake up mad/ panic attacks every night scratching my head searching for lice that aren't there, tonguing teeth to make sure I still have them, so that when I throttle my finger deep inside my skull to see if my mind is still inside it thereby killing myself, I can say I followed the standard operating procedure of losing my goddamn mind. You tell me I'm losing my goddamn mind and to come back to bed. I do this. And we go to sleep.

4) Someone told me that life was better than this. "You should seek life in disparity", they said. "Break rules that bare no meaning. Pro-tip: there is no meaning. Break them all! Kiss coffee into everyone you know and wake them up, so you don't have to be lonely on the road to living your goddamn life and dying. Madness is only mad when there's someone around to witness it." I think that person was a Starbucks barista...

5) I kiss everyone and everything is ok.

Wake Up and Smell the Coffee

Zoe decided that she really needed coffee Tuesday morning. So she drove to her favorite Starbucks in the area. It was the only good place to go for coffee in the suburbs except for this one lit place that was run by Christians. They had the best Chai tea lattes in the world, but still... Christians.

Tyler was so happy to have her back in the state of Illinois that he decided to do the thing he did every morning and ask what coffee she was gonna get. It was a weird ritual where they would ask each other and then they'd take pictures and send them to each other.

It was highly codependent, and Zoe had suddenly grown tired of it. Knowing she was at Starbucks; Tyler messaged her his idea of what she should get. She then blatantly ignored his suggestions.

He mentioned a Sumatra or Yukon thing. It was a Reserves drink and she didn't have that kind of budget at the moment. Tyler Kiosk came from money and wouldn't understand silly things like budgets or the actual weight of failing and getting back up on your own two feet. If he lost his job, his parents would welcome him back for however long he needed.

Zoe had a date she knew she needed to be out by.

After ordering her coffee she sat at the counter next to the pick-up area and took snaps and Instagram videos of the baristas working. She also dutifully sent a picture of her coffee to Tyler saying, "thx for the suggestion! got the Sumatra!" When in reality it was a mocha. The lie was necessary but internally she just didn't know why.

As she continued to take pictures of her coffee and baristas for her Instagram, she wondered whether this bugged them or not-- being in pictures and videos without their own consent. She figured that in a place like Starbucks things like that no longer mattered. Hell, in a place like America, things like that no longer mattered.

She recalled that over like 10 years ago her friend and her were filming at a Starbucks with their digital camera and they were kicked out for having their camera out. They were told there was a no camera policy.

Obviously, phones and apps have forced that rule to change.

Thank fucking God, right?

Like what the fuck are they going to do to impose that one?

Kick everyone out?

It's not like everyone is a black man trying to just sit in peace and wait for their friend. That would just be anarchy to do that to everyone.

God forbid Starbucks treat people with equality...

But that had nothing to do with what she was doing that day.

She decided that no matter what, she would get work done at the Starbucks. Whether it be finding an actual job or writing.

To make sure she'd at least accomplish something, Zoe brought her MacBook Air and her favorite book at the time, Trotsky by Robert Service. As she drank her coffee, she opened her Mac and stared at the book. It was the height of hypocrisy to be reading such a book while drinking an expensive cup of coffee and working on a $1000 Mac. She couldn't help but wonder if her communist ideals had been compromised by her time in San Francisco. She used to imagine she could die for the cause like Trotsky or Che Guevara. Someone with enough essence to commit something and not fuck it up. Follow it through like a normal human being. A good human being. But she was something else. Not quite a fatalist. Not quite a nihilist. Perhaps a person who just felt such loneliness that couldn't be sure she would lay herself down for others or die for her beliefs. She just wasn't sure anymore. So she pushed the book aside and closed her Mac.

She picked up her iPhone to tweet the pictures of her computer and coffee so people thought she was contributing to society in some way but was really trying to think of funny tweets based on observations of people.

At the end though she didn't do any of it.

This is what she did instead:

- Scroll through Facebook.
- Check Twitter.
- Message Tyler.
- Message guy she wanted to date.
- Snapchat Twin Peaks friend.
- Send subtle clues to Twin Peaks friend that she was in his area so he would get the hint to come by.
- Check Facebook again.
- Finish mocha and get a refill with pike (loopholes).
- Listen to 80s and then 90s music on the drive home (it was just The Cure on repeat).

West Coast Boy and the Chicago Girl

West Coast Boy messaged Zoe on Twitter, "What are you up to today?"
"Not much. Just watching Netflix and hanging," she responded but immediately wanted to take back. She knew he was about to ask her to go out somewhere with him.

"That's legit. Want to forget Netflix and catch a movie with me?" asked West Coast Boy.

Zoe instantaneously hit back, "depends on the movie..."

"*Terminator 2* is at The Music Box."

"Rad."

"I'll swing by and we can walk over there together."

Zoe didn't want to let West Coast Boy see her shitty place and Zoe didn't want her roommates to know she was going out with a literary guy, since they both found those people to be weird and that wasn't entirely untrue.

In addition to that, Zoe knew they had a pretty big age gap. He was like 40 and that would just weird her roommates even out more.

At this point it must be explained why a 40-year-old man is referred to as "West Coast Boy." He lived like a nomad. He didn't hold a steady job.

He still wrote poetry. And most importantly, it was his Twitter handle. Zoe finally responded to him, "Nah. I'm good. I'll hop in a Lyft and just meet you there."

"That's cool I guess," said West Coast Boy, "meet me in the lounge 20min before the film starts."

"Cool."

Zoe looked at Twitter and then Facebook for what felt like an hour. She scrolled through one follower's ultra-leftwing political rants and then she scrolled another follower's ultra-rightwing political rant. Both followed fake news, and both hated on hipsters. She imagined that if it weren't for their politics that they'd be a pretty damn fine match for each other.

Then Zoe sat next to Minion and read part of *The Illuminati*. Books like that always amused the hell out of her. Conspiracy theories made her laugh and she loved hearing them. One of her favorite things to do was to try and "out conspiracy theory" a conspiracy theory. If someone doubted that we actually had landed on the moon she would sit there dumbstruck and laugh at the fact that they seriously believed there was a moon. Blowing a conspiracy theorist's mind wasn't a hard thing to do.

Zoe finally got up to get ready to go to see the movie with West Coast Boy at The Music Box Theatre. It wasn't that she didn't want to see a movie at The Music Box. In fact, she was psyched. Almost every weekend she and her roommates went to see movie marathons there and midnight movies at The Logan Theatre. It was just her thing. The feeling of dread she had in the pit of her stomach knowing that one of favorite things to do was probably going to be made awkward by going there with some random dude.

When she got there, West Coast Boy was already in the lounge with a beer. She considered for a second that this theatre had been around since 1929 and then wondered what kind of drink he would've been holding if it was then. She settled on the idea that he probably would've gone with a with a Gin Rickey or an Old Fashioned. Instead it was now and he was drinking an IPA. Zoe wasn't sure if she should walk past him to get a drink at the bar and then join him at his table or or just sit down right away and see if he suggested that she get a drink. While she was wondering this, he got up and hugged her and asked what she was having. She wasn't expecting the hug and just said the first brand of beer she could think of: Angry Orchard. Once she got her drink and they sat down together they attempted to make small talk before the movie. They spoke about the first time they each had seen the film. She watched it on VHS with her brother when she was younger. Zoe remembered that she watched it on a console TV and it was raining. West Coast Boy saw it in a theatre within a mall for a friend's birthday as a teenager. He and his friends got pizza at the food court and had the weird teenage time of their lives. Zoe was seeing just how much their age gap was noticeable. Nothing ages you more than when you tell anecdotes about the first time you've seen certain films.

Both were wearing Apple watches and both went off ten minutes before the film began. They both grabbed their beers and headed towards the actual theatres. She paused for a second to buy her ticket and he pulled a second one out of his pocket.

"Oh. I was thinking I would pay for mine," Zoe sighed in a way that showed she already assumed he was on it.

"No worries," West Coast Boy said as he escorted her into the theatre.

"I'll buy popcorn and candy once we snag seats too," he said before she could object.

West Coast Boy laughed. He was already back to the lobby to grab the candy before his jacket had even hit the seat that he would eventually be sitting in.

He walked back in with a bucket of popcorn and M&Ms. Zoe and West Coast Boy sat and waited for the movie to begin. The previews were almost entirely over by the time they stepped into show and by the time West Coast Boy had returned, the "host" of this special screening was just speaking into an abyss. She never knew why they had hosts. No one ever paid attention unless it was *Rocky Horror Picture Show*.

As the host rambled on into the abyss she remembered that James Cameron also directed a movie called *The Abyss*. Perhaps she'd watch that when she got home.

Zoe was faintly saddened by the fact that they missed the previews. For older pictures, The Music Box always showed the original previews that came with that film. Previews for movies from the 80's and 90's were the best.

"Party foul," Zoe said as West Coast Boy came in with the food. She made sure to say it in a cute way and not a bitchy way. Apparently those were the only two ways a woman's voice can come off as. Her being 5ft tall in a dark theatre with a dude she barely knew made her immediately shield herself with adorableness. She liked the snacks, but she liked the previews better. She also judged his choice of candy for the film. Raisinets were far superior to M&Ms.

"What?" he asked while scooching past people to get to his seat.

"We missed most of previews."

"Damn. I was hoping we'd miss all of them if we hung in the lounge before the show."

"Oh." Zoe said, disheartened.

Zoe felt that the only thing better than seeing a movie at a theater was seeing the trailers for upcoming films. Then the snacks. She was obsessed with trailers and a lot of the time's felt they were almost as exhilarating as the movie she was about to see.

Fuck, some previews for films were better than the actual films they were made for. Zoe often felt like it would be lit if there was an award at the Oscars for "Best Trailer."

She didn't feel a connection with West Coast Boy enough to really go into that. But it is good that they finally got together and that it was to see a movie. You can tell if you're going to click with someone by seeing how they are during a movie or during a road trip.

Movies were far easier.

This theory wasn't wrong though. He brought the wrong snacks. He had little insight into the film. He didn't like previews enough to stick around for them.

She'd had people do worse. One time she went on a date with a guy who, honest to fuck, explained the movie to her as it was going. Another time a guy legit just kept looking to her during the film to see her reactions to certain scenes. The worst, however, was when a guy did all the right things but then pulled his iPhone out mid-movie and started checking Twitter.

The host finally stopped speaking and Arnold would soon be on screen. She preferred the first *Terminator* because it was historical but understood why others loved this one better. The only aspect of the second one she liked was that Sarah Connor was now a badass who no longer had to take someone else's hand to live. Linda Hamilton clearly got jacked for this role. Zoe remembered reading somewhere that James Cameron wrote this film just for her and tailored the entire movie around her character. The only other time she heard of a director doing something like that was when Quentin Tarantino wrote *Kill Bill* for Uma Thurman's 30th birthday.

As the film began, West Coast Boy leaned over and asked her if she knew that Linda Hamilton had a twin sister and that she was used as the stunt double for this movie.

Zoe had no idea whether she should say yes, because she did, so she instead just took a fistful of popcorn and shook her head.

He seemed pleased.

The thing that most people liked about these movies was the nostalgia. For them, the 80's wasn't AIDS, the crack epidemic, and Reaganism. It was cheesy one-liners and synthpop music.

Sarah Conner talking about a fear of a future apocalypse she never saw was a scene that Zoe liked about this movie. It was surreal and matched her thinking.

The future was not set.

She liked seeing the atom bomb that plagued Sarah Connor's nightmares and the laser beam guns that the future fighters had, but also didn't have in the future movies.

 Zoe loved disaster films and therefore loved post-apocalyptic films as well. The Terminator movies were the best at showing what our apocalypse might look like in her opinion, so she enjoyed that best. In a world with Bill Gates and Elon Musk, anything was possible. Honestly, she was shocked that it hadn't happened already. Such a shame. It would've been a rad as fuck way to die.

Oddly though, she felt like if she were in this movie, she'd be able to survive. Zoe didn't want to be in other doomsday films though. Things with zombies or games where people had to fight each other to the death was just not her thing. She also knew that she'd be least likely to survive in a fight to the death. If she were in *The Hunger Games*, her best shot would be to hide and just wait things out in hopes that everyone would somehow all die in their own way leaving her the winner by default. Or she would randomly act suicidal the entire time just to mess with the gamekeeper's head. Pick berries and then get pissed off when they weren't poisonous. Walk directly into unknown smoke, gladly. Things like that. After the movie, West Coast Boy said it was one of his favorite films. He envied the independence of the young John Connor. His heart broke at Sarah's stoic solitude.

Zoe could only comment on the tedious setting and how the film constantly fell back on tropes created by the previous one. She liked the chases though.

She wasn't exactly sure how to part ways with him at that point. She was ready to head out and he seemed to want to hang longer. Zoe wrote a tweet alluding to this awkwardness while hovering near him while he smoked.

The simple tweet read: "Should I Stay or Should I Go." Zoe didn't find this to be her best tweet but was psyched that a lot of people instantly liked it. West Coast Boy liked it too and she had no idea what that meant for their evening.

He continued to linger and smoke, and she considered changing her handle from @NeonTrotsky to @ZoeClark, so she could finally be seen as an adult.

She currently had a cartoon her friend drew for her as her profile pic. Zoe thought it was time to use a real picture of herself at least. Handles could be figured out later. She decided "no time like the present" and took a selfie of herself in front of the theater. When she looked at it, she saw that West Coast boy hopped into frame at the last second. They both laughed and then tried to take a better one of them together. He took the phone to take picture since he had longer arms and was able to take it from far enough where they'd both be in frame. Five bad pictures later, they decided they failed, and he took out another cigarette and offered her one.

As they smoked, West Coast Boy said he was hungry. Zoe suggested Café Pick Me Up. Or Pick Me Up Café. She wasn't sure which way it went, but she knew how to get there, and that the food was good.

They went on foot and enjoyed the Chicago air. He spoke A LOT about Jack Kerouac. She spoke about Bikini Kill. Luckily, they both knew at least a little about the other to keep the conversation flowing.

When they got to the corner where the café was, she could see it was packed. There must've been something sports related that night. It was Wrigleyville. She used to live there. She knew if there were throngs of people it meant a game of some sort. Not just Cubs. She had been living there when the Blackhawks won the Stanley Cup. People went insane and the neighborhood was wild all night. Barriers were preemptively put up in front of the sports bars in case something happened and there were even cops on horses. After they won, the barriers were knocked down and people had flooded into the street. Cops didn't care.

She explained this all to West Coast Boy and he laughed about how sportsy Chicago was. She couldn't deny it, but she also tried to explain that it had an interesting culture if one looked far enough back. Before she could explain any further, they were taken to a booth to eat. Zoe looked at the wall next to it, flooded with pictures and things random people wrote and put up there. She found a drawing that her cartoon friend did. It was a drawing of himself with a Chai Tea Latte and had a thought bubble that said, "If at first you don't succeed, chai, chai again..."

Zoe pointed this out to West Coast Boy, but she could tell that he didn't find the dorkiness as amusing as she did. Instead, he wanted to tell her all about his travels and his writing and what he wanted to do with his life.

When the waitress came with the menus, he said we didn't need them. He ordered two coffees and one slice of cherry pie. He knew Zoe had a *Twin Peaks* tattoo and looked into her eyes for approval after the waitress left. Zoe didn't vibe with that kind of behavior and wasn't in the mood for caffeine that late at night. But she saw in his eyes like he was like a dog with a bone, so she smiled and asked, "How did you know I was just about to order that?"

He was all smiles. They stayed for approximately 1.5 hours there and most of it was spent awkwardly trying to split the slice of pie without looking weird. Eventually she just gave up and after two bites said she wasn't that hungry. He gladly finished and then jumped up to pay at the register before she could take her own money out. She grabbed her jacket and followed him outside where they again lingered awkwardly. Zoe officially was ready to go and ordered a Lyft to come pick her up. She made an excuse that her roommates got annoyed if she came back to the apartment too late. He understood and said he totally got it.

When the Lyft arrived, he guided her to the door and then paused for a strange amount of time with his hand one hand on the door. He eventually said, "fuck it" and bent down to kiss her. She clumsily kissed back and then got into the car to go home. She thought about how awkward her first kiss was when she was in high school and the feeling that when she was older kissing would become less weird.

It hadn't.

Semi-Rad, Semi-Sad

After what felt like an eternity, Zoe finally got a job working as a barista in Ravenswood and a place to live in Roscoe Village. This was an ideal situation for her because she was able to earn enough for rent but also have enough free time to devote to her writing. Having two other roommates wasn't ideal, but it was nothing like the hectic place where she had lived in San Francisco. She could deal with this. Besides, they worked day jobs and she got the apartment to herself for long periods of time.

That morning, she woke up to check her account balance in her checking account on her MacBook.

Only 27% battery remaining, and it was several years old. So she'd have to do it quickly.

Only $84 in funds...

She quickly calculated how much she was going to need for rent that month and a dress she needed to buy on Sunday for a baby shower and the gift wrapping paper she'd have to do for a gift she'd have to buy and other bullshit like that. Her sister-in-law was having her first baby, so she understood why it was so important to her. But still, it was a lot of money to spend just to make a brotherfucker happy.

With all those excess purchases, she wouldn't be able to go out for coffee for weeks. Even with the next few paychecks she'd be getting from her old job, she'd never be able to cover all of that and fun stuff for herself.

She was going to stay at home and conserve the stuff she had left.

Her only fear was that she might run out and be forced to siphon off her roommate's giant barrel of Folgers that had been sitting on the kitchen counter for what seemed to have been months. She couldn't decide what was worse: that she'd have to resort to drinking stale coffee or that it was Folgers? In a weird and dark moment, she remembered how The Manson Family killed an heiress from the Folgers family and smiled. Abigail Folger. Oddly, she wasn't the least famous person in that house that died that twisted night but she was the most forgotten. She knew it was dark and fucked up but so was she. The crime was horrific, and no human being deserves to die in in such a perverse and unaffected manner. It didn't just kill a fuck ton of famous people, it killed the innocence of the 60's. While thinking all of this, Zoe felt unshaken by her own darky and twisty thoughts. The song "Hollywood Forever Cemetery" by Father John Misty started ringing in her ears. She hummed to it and felt it was pretty funny how much she hated Folgers and wondered if that was why Abigail Folger was the least talked about victim when people discussed the Manson Family Murders.

A dog walked by the window of her apartment out of nowhere and she thought about how simple it would to be a dog. Just blissfully wander around life unaware of mortality or money or shit like that.

In some weird *Sex and the City* kind of way she wanted to write it off to some sassy thought or sexual epiphany that could go in some half-rate column but instead all she could do is get up and watch *Bridesmaids* and wonder if her life was ever going to get any better.

These things tend to turn out okay for some people, right?

You read these stories everyday about artists who had nothing and somehow made it in the end. Patti Smith and Kathleen Hanna came to mind.

It kind of sounded like rags to riches bullshit to her and Zoe, being a capitalist hater, tried not to buy into such things. But still, she was wondering if it was something that could ever happen.

Instead, she closed her computer and ignored a Facebook invite her roommate sent her three days ago for some pool party on top of some guy's high rise in the loop. Weird when the roommate could've just popped into her room and invited her. She wouldn't have gone anyhow. Again, capitalism. Also, Zoe hated forced social interactions with people she didn't know and didn't want to.

Roommate lived that kind of glamorous lifestyle though. The kind that only trust funders and influencers get to.

One time her roommate even invited her to hangout on some Turkish guy's yacht. Roommate had only met him like two days prior. That's just the kind of girl she was. Zoe could never be that. She either didn't care enough or didn't think she belonged with people like that. After all, she was just a dorky writer.

Instead, Zoe went to some bumfuck town in Iowa to visit her boyfriend who was completely clueless as to where he wanted to go in life. Their romance was new, but they saw each other rarely and this suited them. Their relationship was open in a way where she could date other people, but her boyfriend would always be hers.

Maybe she should've gone to roommate's boujee thing.

Maybe she should've finally started hanging out with the Chicago artists who wanted to connect with her now that she was there.

Maybe she should've taken that start-up job that her roommate suggested.

Or maybe she'd grab the half-drunk decaf coffee she left in the bathroom the night before and reheat it so she could have something to help perk up as she watched *Bridesmaids* in preparation for the baby shower. It seemed to be the same mood of a baby shower and she needed to laugh.

If You Stop Typing,
All Progress will be Lost

Zoe spent the four hours staring at the screen on her MacBook Air. On the screen there it said "YOU FAILED" in white on a red backdrop in Helvetica. She had screenshotted it from when she was trying to write back in San Francisco. She always preferred criticism over compliments. Pain more than pleasure. Zoe's heart even settled more when she lost something rather than found it. There was no excitement without those things. No exigency or cathartic pleasure when the bad went away. She often referred to herself as a "pessimistic optimist." A person fully comfortable with negative outcomes because they were expecting it. A person who was in sheer shock when things went right.

She kept that screenshot for that reason. It gave her peace. Not just the words but the look of it too. The aesthetic of it was beautiful in a way that words couldn't describe.

The font popped. It was fresh af.

The background for some reason felt warm not alarming and the words weren't threatening but affirming.

This has absolutely nothing to do with what she was doing or the story of her life.

It's just interesting to note that Zoe was the kind of person who has "YOU FAILED" written in front of her and she just never seemed to mind.

Her failure to make money was something other people seemed to mind though. Tyler planned a hangout with Zoe for them to get drinks the next night but he decided they should also get pizza and then go back to her apartment and watch *Speed*. He was the only friend she had left who was willing to make compromises on things to do when she was stuck on a budget.

She thought this was great until she got an email notifying her that her Spotify payment failed. This made her finally check out her bank account and find out that she legit only had ten dollars in her account.

Fuck, right?

Forget drinks. She couldn't afford to even buy a small pizza if she wanted. She had nothing. She was shocked her Netflix account was still somehow working.

Now she had to go through the embarrassing effort of once again telling her friend, who had a normal adult job, that she couldn't do the simple things that a normal adult typically could do because she wanted to be a writer.

Instead of having a few hours of watching *All the President's Men* before she slept, she had to message her sister on what to say to her friend.

She gave no insight whatsoever. Zoe's sister just simply told her it would get better.

Zoe sighed and said, "I know," but it still destroyed her in a tiny way. It was the sort of feeling you only got as a kid when you fell on your back and got the wind knocked out of you. It was fleeting but for a few seconds the sensation was still there.

She wrote on her notepad app an idea of what to send Tyler the next day. An excuse instead of the actuality that she was broke. He would judge immediately if she told the truth. So she decided to lie. Something along the lines of "I'm trying to stay healthy...I'm gonna eat a salad and try to rest for once... maybe we can do that Netflix Party like we did back when I was in San Francisco if I'm not too tired..."

She saved it for later and messaged Tyler other things for a few hours just to make him think things were chill in her life.

Her humiliation would have to wait until the next morning.

Perfectly Post Modern

None of Zoe's writing was taken very seriously and wasn't widely published. She always found excuses to not submit it anywhere. She spoke about her writing with her friends often but had never shown it to anyone. But she did write. She wrote a lot. She even wrote an entire novel in a single evening once. It was accidentally deleted during a computer reboot though, so there was no real proof it existed. She liked to think she was like Kafka. An author who had great works that no one read and were thrown in a fireplace. It was probably all amazing. The writing of his that could never be read.

But Zoe did not think she was some great writer that would be discovered after her death. From either sluggishness or severe depression, she couldn't bring herself to write. And when she could, anxiety and chronic procrastination kicked in just enough to prevent her from submitting her writing. Zoe thought she might feel better by this age and try to write more but she knew she was lying to herself.

Zoe was thirty. She had written her first poem when she was sixteen. It shocked her even to this day. Her teacher found it on her desk and loved it and then told her to submit it to a specific journal and then it got published.

Things weren't that simple anymore.

Zoe chewed the cap from her pen. It tasted like plastic and earwax. She forgot she had kept her pen behind her ear the weird taste was a result of that. She spat the cap out like it was gum and was disgusted with herself. She ran to the bathroom to use mouthwash. While she was swishing out the bad taste, Elle from New York Facebooked her: "Yo, what up?"

Zoe returned from bathroom.

"Not much. I was just brushing my teeth. What's up?"

Zoe didn't want to go into the whole pen incident and thought that brushing her teeth would lead to less questions than using mouthwash.

Ell hit back, "Going to that lit party tonight at that warehouse. Should be pretty rad. You should come."

Zoe didn't really feel like going to a party, but she knew she should because Elle was only there for a few days and then she'd go to New Orleans. Zoe was already supposed to hook up with her in Andersonville for a poetry reading the night before. She couldn't ditch her again. Zoe was terrible at telling people when she didn't want to do something. Instead, she'd say yes and then find an excuse to bail at the last minute. It was a flaw she knew she had and she listed it as something she should work on in therapy.

This made Zoe seem like she was a just a baby, like John had said before he died. But he would do the exact same thing too. That's just how some writers are.

And Here it is...

After almost two years and three months of not seeing each other, Zoe messaged Cooper via Snapchat and insisted that they finally get together.

During the summer months they used to spend whole nights at a donut shop on Northwest Highway. They'd drink stale coffee and talk about movies and politics and David Lynch. Occasionally *Mad Men* would be mentioned. She'd test the waters to see how radically leftist he was and he'd test the waters to see if she wanted to fuck. Neither were on the same page but the conversations were too damn fine to miss out on. Even during that weird time when she lived in San Francisco they kept up on the messaging at least. Both always begging the other to come out. Neither of them had the follow through to go that far for each other though. But when she finally came back to the Windy City both were more than thrilled to try and pick up their donut hangouts again.

As for the conversations they had, they met somewhere in the middle. She'd keep things strictly liberal and maintain a light flirtation bordering on legit consideration. Now that she was back, she considered it even more than she had in the past. When they'd first met it was just funny when he hit on her because he was so boyish and at least five years younger than she was. It seemed beyond wrong to do anything though. But now that he was far more grown and had matured into a legit man, it wasn't totally out of the bounds of reality. Of course, this notion went completely went out the window when he sent her a Snap of him wearing a pink Kanye hat and smoking a vape.

I guess some things never change…

Before the night that they would hang she suddenly felt a surge of regret.

This is something that introverts and depressed people will all understand but everyone else will think, "WTF."

Zoe was tired and depressed and wasn't sure if coffee was the thing for her at the moment. But then she did the thing that introverts must do at times. She threw on music and did her best to hype herself up. After several Father John Misty songs, she started to think maybe it was a good idea to see Coop. It had been a while and she needed some fresh air, so she thought "who the fuck cares… I'll go." She threw on the outfit that she was dead set on wearing and then got pissed. It was going to be her favorite torn high-waist jeans with a Beyoncé t-shirt tucked into them. All she needed to complete the look were her sandals, but she couldn't find them anywhere. Her goddamn roommate took them, and she knew it.

That's the problem with living with other bitches, they just take your shit without asking. Fuck, her roommate was well over a foot taller than she was. How the hell did she even fit into Zoe's sandals? The whole thing just boggled her, and it would become a thing that wouldn't let go of for a long time.

She sighed and changed her clothes, feeling hopeless once again. She eventually got up and put on black skinny jeans with a white shirt and black American Apparel hoodie. Her converse would match with that and she wouldn't feel as pissed at her roommate if she was able to look good in a different outfit.

When she hit the highway to the far away suburbs she got sleepy and turned on all the new music from Bleachers. She laughed in the car thinking of all possible scenarios her being someone who was capable of making music. Or her being the inspiration for someone else writing these songs and then them explaining the origin story to other people who were also famous. It totally upset her that the idea of being famous sounded so much more fun than writing, but it was making her happy, so she turned the music louder and enjoyed the ride.

When she got to the merge sections between the two highways, she brought herself back down to reality and accepted the fact that the next few hours would probably be relegated to discussing hip hop and they would probably never discuss her love of bad hipster music. They were only five years apart in age but they were from two quite different generations. Together they hated baby boomers. But apart they were on two truly unusual teams.

But that was life, and she knew that it was part of their compromise as friends. They'd ignore the differences and just try to have fun. All friends make strange little compromises when it comes to hang outs.

At this point in the story, I will have to really assert that Zoe was not a pretentious hipster, but she was a pessimist. People rarely fit with her perfectly. Even her fellow pessimist, Tyler, annoyed the ever-loving hell out of her at times.

When she pulled up at the donut shop she messaged Cooper, "Here."

She didn't hear the notification that went on her phone earlier when she was blasting music, but after sending him text that she was there, she saw that he messaged five minutes earlier: "across the street at the gas station. hit me up when you're here."

She laughed and looked over and immediately recognized his pink Kanye hat and denim jacket that she thought he looked adorable in. Zoe considered shouting or going across the street to say it to his face, but she knew in a few minutes he'd join her over in the parking lot of the donut shop.

She used this opportunity to run into the shop and quickly order so she could get her coffee and run to the bathroom before he was in there. She also wanted to race to get to the seats in the good spot of the shop that they typically hung at. They were corner seats that actually made it possible to face something other than the donuts or TV that was constantly playing a show called *F Troop* on repeat. Perhaps there were nightly marathons of that show on some cable TV channel but it wasn't something she would've known. She hadn't watched actual cable in years. It was to the point that commercials actually make her squirm. Streaming services were something that made her happy. She even laughed a few times at the shop owner that they should consider getting Netflix, only for them to laugh back at her about how they "wouldn't get Square so what makes her think they'd even consider getting streaming services for their tiny TV hanging in the corner?" Cooper came into the shop and sat where they usually sat, even though she was still in the bathroom. She liked that he finally had taken a liking to that spot because it was the only place where they could face each other instead of awkwardly sitting next to each other.

She came out shortly and saw that he already ordered. When he saw Zoe, he leapt up hugged her in a way that felt gentle and warm. She could tell that he wanted to go longer and sometimes she could feel that he wanted to pick her up but she respected the fuck out of the fact that he didn't. She respected it so much that she kind of wanted the hug to go longer too, but didn't want to give him the wrong idea.

After two whole hours of "black as midnight on a moonless night" coffee and borderline savage jokes about the school shootings, a strange man walked into the empty donut shop and walked towards them with his hand deep in his pockets.

She knew she was crazy, but she totally got flashbacks of the *Zodiac* movie with Jake Gyllenhaal. This dude was almost definitely the fucking Zodiac. She could easily see him attacking her quickly and her boy struggling but ultimately failing to save her because he was small, like her. She would die, but he would live because for some reason the Zodiac always managed to only kill the women but didn't always finish off the dudes.

She whispered this to Cooper, so he knew why she was staring at creepy guy. He agreed that there was no way that he'd be able to help her but did find it funny because the first confirmed couple killed by Zodiac was a girl who was out with a younger dude.

They both laughed and then saw that the guy was heading into the bathroom and not over to them.

It clearly had been a long night.

A few more hours of coffee and Zoe knew she was finally too tired to stay anymore or feign interest in gangster movies or Kanye.

He walked her to her black Mini Cooper because he always did after hangouts. Before the warm goodnight she knew she was about to get from Cooper, they noticed that the creepy guy was an Uber driver from the stickers on his windshield. On the passenger's side it looked like there were two sticky looking rubber cloves.

She pointed at them and laughed, "oh shit better call OJ," and her boy laughed with her.

They hugged and said goodbye and she drove back to the city thinking about how someday she would totally make it. Maybe he'd finally do his hip hop thing or director thing and maybe she'd be a writer or musician.

Who the fuck knows?

She woke up the next day and quite ironically the first thing that was newly added to Netflix was *The People v. O.J. Simpson: American Crime Story*.

Subject on Where We Land on the Tertiary-Extinction Timeline, Paleontologists Will Use Us To Resurrect Prehistoric Predators

She stayed inside for three whole days watching Kaiju films and ordering from Doordash. Occasionally she went to her balcony and drank a beer. One of her roommates just moved out and she was both happy and sad about this. She'd have to take on more of the rent, but she'd also have a room free to potentially use as an office. One less person to pretend to like. One more room to pay for.

Life be like that sometimes.

When the roommate moved out, Zoe was pretty damn sure some of her books went missing but decided to just shrug it off. This was why she hated living with other people.

Tyler lived alone and this sometimes made her jealous, but she also knew that this made him really lonely. So lonely that now he has made it a weekly thing to drive all the way to her apartment just to hang out with her, even if it was just for a quick hour.

On this day he decided to come over to drink on her balcony with her and talk about all the films. They drank Angry Orchard as the sky changed from orange to sort of black. It was the city, and a carnival was happening across the street, so no darkness ever really happened there. Just colors that could be described as either warm or cold. As Zoe bitched to Tyler about the old roommate, she felt a bite and realized it was mosquito season. She drank and thought about how much she was going to itch later and then how long mosquitos had existed on this planet.

A sudden mass extinction event occurred about 66 million years ago, killing everything from dinosaurs to plankton. Three-quarters of the world's animal life wiped out in an instant. A flash of an asteroid came with abrupt change. Something called "impact winter" ensued and then from those ashes came us. Yet even then, mosquitos thrived.

They decided to go inside and watch *Jurassic Park* because it was just so on point with her thinking. Also, Tyler seemed to want to do whatever Zoe wanted to do. Scientists discovered an ancient mosquito encased in amber and could clone dinosaurs. This being late capitalism, the only thing they could think to do with such a discovery was make an amusement park.

Sigh.

The possibilities.

What could have been?

Could it happen?

Imagine an ancient mosquito enclosed by amber being discovered beneath twelve feet of permafrost. Scientists would of course use it to resurrect dinosaurs using advanced techniques in cybernetics. Instead of frog DNA, neuroscientists could give the dinosaurs superhuman intelligence. These prehistoric predators would seek out human life and demolish it in frightening and previously unconsidered ways.

During a time period of intense trepidation and eschatological fear you would project positive emotions onto people's faces.

Their faces would reflect the positive emotions so intensely that it would discharge gigantic ion beams toward the moon and destroy the moon. Perhaps someone would drift up emotionally in the sky like a cliché metaphor about a child's balloon.

Where the moon once was would be a giant void that resembled a fish tank from far away.

Zoe imagined floating in this void like an iridescent goldfish.

Her face would be distorted by the convex surface of the void and she would feel depressed about not being able to project positive emotions.

She would feel better about not being destroyed by prehistoric predators as the lingering earthbound humans were hunted down and thoroughly annihilated.

She would live in the cold void until the day she would swim toward the sun with her skin melting until she resembled an abstract painting.

She immediately picked up her phone to write all of these thoughts down, but when she began Tyler paused the film and ask, "is everything okay?" He did this every time she picked up her phone. Like this time was set aside for him and only him. There was a part of him she could tell that felt that he "won" when she moved back to the city. But their friendship had nothing to do with it and she would never be able to break that to him. Their bond was fading and she was resenting these hangouts more and more. Him watching her watch the movies they picked out. Studying her every reaction in a frightening and previously unconsidered way. When they lived states apart her couldn't do this and she could mentally check out.

Now he was here and it was too much. She imagined again, floating in the void and wishing that perhaps she could volunteer her DNA to create these superhuman Dinosaurs. The ancient mosquitos encased by amber had to exist somewhere. And somehow, this resentment had to end. Even if it meant the world ending with it.

Live by the Sun, Love by the Moon

Zoe's boyfriend sat on top of a train for a while, staring out into the great fields of Iowa, like a night watchman on a metal perch. Glancing up at the sky and breathing in the brisk. Converting cold air into warmth for his already numbed fingers. He wore fingerless gloves so he could use his iPhone, but the cold made this idea seem incredibly stupid. He decided to take a book out of his backpack to get his mind off the cold. He pulled out *Beggars of Life* by Jim Tully and got pissed off.

It was that kind of writing that got him in this position in the first place. The idea of being a man of the rails to prove himself seemed kind of beautiful. He saw how rich kids travelled and why they did, but he decided he was different. For him, this wasn't a mission of self-discovery, it was a way of life. He wanted to live on as little as possible while experiencing the most things possible. Zoe found this laughable and he knew she'd mock him when she picked him up later.

The burning in the back of his throat was inflamed with each inhale. His nose red. It was hard not being resentful of writers who made living like this sound exciting. There were other guys near the tracks gathered by a fire. He could have joined the others, but he had this defunct urge to be alone with his thoughts. So there he was. Hours wasted. Trying to clutch onto each and every moment. Reexamining his life, like we all do from time to time. Hoping to inspire himself to seize the day. Or night, as it was. Freezing cold.

At the same time, his mind travelled far and away. Miles away from there. Like the adventurous carefree guy he once was. Always going through the same cycle of regret.

His father.

The road.

The confliction.

Zoe.

Her eyes forever etched in the sky like a constellation. Without the road their love would not be possible.

Since the beginning of time, seafarers and tramps found direction thanks to those stars, but with each upward glance he felt lost.

Her lips never to be touched by his again. Her hand never to be held by him. Her books to never be read. His dreams never to be realized.

Sometimes it was all just too much and he had no idea how to make things right between them.

The time between summer and winter has a way of making one self-reflective.

The leaves of autumn fall and decay into a kind of darkened sentimentality. The bereavement of the earth is in full view for a season and the nature that once hid the decomposing and remorse recedes. The sins of all us men on display. It's a beautiful time. It was Zoe's favorite season, and he wasn't able to spend it with her. They made agreements before about keeping things open, but it was killing him to swipe through her Instagram each day and see her doing things with other friends and go on what looked like dates.

*****

He'd stare out at that sky forever if he could. Transfixed by the glittering luminescence above. Every star twinkling with truth. Knowing that it was his destiny to be amongst them. Just wanting to be in the presence of something that connected him to every great traveler out there. Feeling small in the scope of something so big.

But loud music coming from a black mini-cooper in the distance and broke his train of thought.

Radley leapt from his metal perch to see the commotion. Found that as usual, Zoe was tired and wanted him to drive all the way back to Chicago.

The words, "Time to lean, Time to clean," were shouted from the train. He wasn't done working yet and Zoe would have to wait in the car until he was officially done. Slavedriver of a boss, the dick was.

He was a numbers man. Believed in the American dream. Brought up to believe in Capitalism and that if you worked hard enough you could be a millionaire, just like Steinbeck said. He didn't believe in the frivolities or "fru-fru" as he called it. He had one simple rule: when you were at work, you worked. If you didn't feel like working, he'd find somebody who did, and you could find yourself a new job. And you couldn't ever use the excuse that "there was no work to be done," because in the train-yards, there was always work to be done.

Radley told him once that we were allotted a certain number of breaks. Told him it was union policy. Boss called Radley a pinko and threw a tool in his general direction. So much for all that literature from Haymarket books that Zoe had given him.

Guess people really don't give a shit about that kind of stuff anymore... He didn't take this personally, mind you. For some fucked up reason, Radley rather enjoyed the tension. It reminded him of his father. It reminded him of life before he became a statistic.

*****

The boss came over and said they had to do a rail switch for an oncoming freighter. Radley obliged and headed to it, knowing Zoe was growing impatient in the car.

It's amazing how quickly one is conditioned to oblige and mindlessly go about tasks. Like we were preordained monkeys on a mission. We could make iPhones, design digital realities, and brew pumpkin spiced lattes, but we couldn't fight the system. Only wars in faraway lands.

The reality of that all made Radley sick, but that's why he did this. Why he took this job. Why he never returned home after meeting Zoe. When you find out your life is a "matrix" who could return home to the hustle and bustle? He certainly couldn't ever face his father again, recognizing the white-collar drone he was. Besides, he'd never forgive him for leaving school. He was supposed to be getting his PhD in Philosophy at Berkley. Instead, he was back in Iowa working at a rail yard.

Radley latched onto the ground-throw and pulled it in time for the giant freighter to switch tracks right before his eyes. It was like a behemoth. Just so big. And the ground trembled beneath it. Capitalism would live another day.

He sat beside the tracks at the ground-throw and waited for the miles-long-train to pass so that he could switch the rails again, lest they have an incident right out of some crappy Ayn Rand novel.

Moments like these made him love his job. He was technically working, but he had time for his thoughts. But with Zoe waiting on him he was just in a hurry to get everything done as fast as possible. As the train went by, he wondered what the other guys did with themselves during those long bouts of inert silence. But it was an exercise in futility and he always returned inward. Sometimes he'd gaze at the stars. Sometimes he'd jot down his thoughts on an aged legal pad. Tonight, he thought about the night he left home.

*****

Zoe encouraged him to go on the road again and find himself. She had the same feeling of wanderlust that he had. But she had a certain amount of follow-through that he lacked.

Radley still remembered the feeling of excitement he had when he sat with Zoe and Macky in that diner and made an itinerary for their trip East.

He still remembered telling his father that he was leaving the PhD program and coming back to Iowa. It wasn't meant to be a permanent thing. He just honestly had no idea when he would return to the program or if he ever would. So Radley just said he was leaving. He wasn't happy.

He remembered telling his father that he felt lost in the world. That his privileged and sheltered life could never bring him any future. Radley had seen life through frosted glass and televisions. But he wanted to live it. Walled off in some gated community prevented him from growing and there was no other sensible remedy but to wander until he had found himself.

"You're just running away," his father said, "being a man means not running away."

His father just couldn't understand. He came from Belarus. He lived on the other side of the wall. Literally, he was a part of the USSR. He didn't have the privilege that smothered Radley so much. Radley envied him that. But he couldn't connect Radley's need to be on the road with anything but escaping from responsibility.

"Radley, we came to this country so you can learn and go to good college," his father yammered on, "You repay us by becoming a bum?"

Radley never forgot the conflicted feeling of shame and anticipation he had that night when he left. He knew that his father would feel this way because what reasonable parent didn't? His dad was much more like the American parents than he would ever want to admit. Obsessed with college and the status quo. His father wanted Radley so earnestly to follow the rules of society.

Radley didn't know how to convince him that this is what he wanted to do with his life.

So Radley just left. Convinced that one day his happiness and fulfillment in this life would prove him wrong.

*****

Screeching and clanking echoed in the distance and brought him back to the train yard. Seems like Radley was always the only one affected by those cumbersome sounds. Then again, he was always the only one lost in his own mind.

The final cars of the freighter passed and he flipped the ground-throw to switch the rails. The hairs on his face may have grown a little longer in the time he spent waiting. But these days all he had was time to wait. Radley climbed the frosty ladder, his fingerless gloves damning him to the exposure again, and hopped into Zoe's car. He no longer had to expose himself to the brisk air or hide in his thoughts for the few hours it took to get to Chicago.

Radley thought of the beat travelers who took to the road, back when the road still meant something. How so many boys so badly had wanted to be explorers in search of something new and adventurous.

He was once one of them. Days spent fantasizing about toiling the earth and being an explorer. He recalled the hunger to see new things, but now he was starving for more. The romantic notion that life could be nothing more than a knapsack and the horizon as his home was gone.

But even then, he was conflicted. Radley was afraid of the unknown. Scared of what life would be like if he couldn't predict it. But the person he had become, scared him more. He told Zoe the whole way home how he once frolicked in fields. Sipped on coffee every time, like it was the first time. Cried because he realized that it was beautiful to just stand in the rain. Was joyful at the thought of the future.

And that one morning he woke up and was on an express train to death. Zoe worried about things like this all the time and it seeped into Radley's consciousness like inception. She would insist that capitalism was ripping her life to shreds. But it was just depression. Depression mixed with capitalism.

But before she came into his life, he was afraid. Afraid of the day when he would have to choose between what is and what could be. A job or life. She guided him. But there he was, alone. Paying the penance for living a life less ordinary. He considered living a life less ordinary but in one place with her.

*****

Radley knew he didn't want to be in that train yard. Some faceless grunt. His hunger wasn't satisfied there. But his resources were exhausted. And at the time he felt beat. But as he stared at Zoe driving, he found direction once again.

He could see himself months later. He could see himself in one place. He could see himself going on the road again with her. The stars would be the only thing to guide them.

He sat there pondering his future and continued to stare out. Out upon the unending wheat of Iowa.

Out upon the rising sun.

Out upon the stars that were no longer visible but were always there beside him.

Upon the road in the distance, beyond the train yard. Lustful and black.

He told Zoe to pull over so he could drive a bit. He leapt into the front seat and made fun of the fact that she always had it so close to the steering wheel and needed to move it back. He fixed it and then drove them both to Chicago. His eyes towards the horizon. Towards the road. Towards the passing men readying the train. Thinking of autumn and the leaves. And how he wouldn't miss another autumn with Zoe.

The leaves would die like everything else did. But not without showing their many colors and beauty. They would dry up and become compost for harvest. He wanted to rake leaves and jump in them with Zoe. He even imagined being a father for a split second and then freaked out.

These were no longer thoughts but life plans that he'd need to discuss with Zoe later. She was already pissed and tired from waiting so long for him to finish work.

Our Relationship Status Right Now:
It's Caffeinated

Zoe stayed up late at night with Radley discussing what they should do the next day now that he was in the city to stay.

- Coffee at My Half of the Sky?
- Starbucks in the suburbs?
- That one cool coffee place that used to be another cool coffee place?

The fact that coffee consumed her life didn't exactly surprise her and it definitely didn't surprise him. She had a cup of coffee everywhere she went. From the first time he saw her to the conversation they had about coffee last night.

At first it was for fun and novelty for her. For him, it was just another one of her quirks that made her the kind of manic pixie dream girl he'd seen in movies his whole life. He didn't know yet that she was a *manic-depressive* dream girl until they finally moved in together.

For Zoe, coffee was all about the caffeine but now was was all about the price. For someone who was pursuing writing and living on little to nothing it was the ultimate cheap activity.

Yes, she was a professor, but they were rather undervalued in today's society, and that's something that really needed to be addressed at some point.

Whenever Zoe wasn't drinking coffee at work, she was drinking it to stay awake to write when she got home or on weekends. It felt fun and hipstery to sit in a coffee shop and talk with friends and hangout for hours.

She wouldn't tell her friends that it was due to money though. Although she had no problem with the image of being a "starving" artist, she hated to actually admit that she was.

People would never understand...

They would think she was going overboard on the brand that she didn't even know she'd made...

Some people even confronted her on her truly clear addiction. What most people didn't know though, was that most of the time she was just ordering decaf.

Wild, right?

Like yeah, she threw in the actual caffeine occasionally but due to anxiety and manic depression she was scared beyond all fuck to rock that boat. She didn't hide her mental illness, but she didn't want people to know just how much it changed her life.

It all started like a gazillion years ago when she first had a manic meltdown. Up until then she thought she was someone who just got depressed occasionally and that she was fine. Depression was something she could handle. Mania was just something wilder and scarier.

Her therapist urged her to change her lifestyle completely and eventually Zoe did. But to throw away coffee would be to throw away her entire relationship with the outside world. It was the main thing she did with friends.

So now she orders decaf three times out of five.

She planned to slowly reintroduce it into her system again soon but for now she just wanted to get a grip on life. She also desperately wanted to make Radley happy and show him cool parts of the city that was her home.

They picked a cute place in Humboldt Park called CC Ferns Coffee Bar & Spirits. It served the best chai in the city and had cool coffee cocktails. One could describe it as casual but classy. Hipstery but intimate. The ambience of that coffee shop was something she'd never seen before so she knew Radley would like it. Going to CC Ferns was like being transported to someone's basement but that person had a 50's Cuban theme and they just happened to be serving coffee. Vintage artwork. Cigar cases. Tin ceiling and soft surfaces. It was a small and cozy space where you could legit hear someone whisper over the noise of the espresso machine.

If the chatter of the hipsters hanging with their lattes on the soft vintage furniture was too much, there were outdoor tables to in front that made Radley think of Istanbul. Zoe couldn't imagine it since she'd never been. But she definitely felt like stepping into that coffee shop was like stepping out of America and she loved it.

Going Nowhere

After some talking into, Zoe began to consider the idea of becoming a professor herself. She already had a PhD in Russian history and Radley convinced her she shouldn't let it go to waste. Funny since he almost completed his PhD and let his go to waste.

Now he worked at a tech startup that will remain unnamed.

Her first day teaching at the college near Little Italy began the same way that she thought it would. She got up and dressed way too chill for the circumstances.

She took a bus and long L ride to the school and she was exhausted. When she got to the school she got confused for a student several times.

She didn't bring enough coffee.

She didn't bring enough Xanax.

This was just all shit to keep in mind for the second day, Radley later told her. Nothing to get too worried about.

Let's face it though...she kind of liked being confused for a student. She was thirty and being mistaken for twenty-three. Not bad.

Something about it just made her feel better about herself and that made it easier to not feel like she was sacrificing her hopes and dreams of becoming a writer. Lots of cool writers had normal jobs like that before hitting it big.

She had to upward strive or whatever therapists said and take confidence in the fact that she was only thirty, which for some reason they kept telling her was still young. Her lifestyle was beginning to get out of hand before she made the big decision to finally get that normal job.

She was depressed and anxious all the time.

She was spending way too much time on Netflix and she never wrote the way she said she would.

Perhaps by having a serious routine that demanded her to be more awake and vigilant would inspire her to work more.

Or perhaps it would replace her love of writing all together.

Or depress her by taking away all of her free time.

One can't predict how things are going to unfold. But one can make a list of intentions and hope that they come through.

There were her intentions:

- Work the two semesters
- Make money
- Pay bills
- Go to more poetry readings
- Do short weekend trips to make Radley happy

She also considered the idea of possibly becoming wildly famous on Instagram or Twitter but didn't bother to list it out because she knew it just wasn't going to happen.

She could perhaps live tweet some of her courses or become someone who wildly dissed politicians or something.

It was all up for grabs and she was trying to make herself feel chill with it.

Life be like that sometimes...

Watch More Sunrises than Netflix

Zoe felt like a train wreck every morning and didn't really know what to do about that.

In theory coffee would fix everything, but now that life had grown more difficult, simple caffeine just wouldn't help.

She had an internet friend from New Jersey that she grew quite fond of who was allergic to coffee. In a deep and concerned way this freaked the ever-loving fuck out of her.

It sounded like something that could totally happen though, so that sucked.

I mean legit...some people can't have peanuts, chocolate, hazelnuts...he couldn't have coffee.

Them's the breaks.

It sucked. Just damn...fuck.

She spent most of her week working on lectures and wondering about who she really was in life.

She yearned to be considered great in something. She used to lie about it and say she was doing everything to reach a higher form in life.

Engels would discuss the family unit in this way. The more communist work...the higher form the family reaches.

She thought this was a way she could describe her life.

She wanted a higher form.

But when the night always ended, she just wanted to know why people didn't love her and if she really was even good at anything.

She wanted to be a great writer, but she just didn't write enough. She wanted to be a great historian with a PhD, but she realized that her PhD meant nothing to her. She wanted to be an expert at something but still wasn't. They gave it to her anyways.

Who can just be an expert like in *Greys Anatomy* or *Mad Men*?

All she wanted to do now was talk about *Mad Men*, so she hit up her Mad Men Buddy. This was the same person as her David Lynch buddy.

The whole story surrounding that friendship was a mad and difficult one so we really shouldn't get into it, but what's important is that she went on Snapchat and hit that guy up.

They went to that donut shop that she loved, but she knew deep down he just wasn't a fan of it. But it was still just their thing.

She appreciated that most of her friends let her dictate when and where their hangouts would be. Apparently not all people were like this.

She surrounded herself with good people.

This is something important in life.

Finding good people and keeping those good people around you.

If you find a good person, for the love of fuck don't let them go...even if you do have countless nights where you think of suicide or if you sometimes abuse that friendship, apologize for that shit in the morning.

If they truly are good people, they'll get it and love you anyhow.

So anyways she hit up that one dude who was a good person. They met at the shop and spoke for five hrs.

She wanted to dive into Don Draper, but he had his own concerns. So they tackled that instead.

The same two guys always worked behind the counter at that place.

A young guy who was always stoned to fuck and an older guy with a mustache who reminded her of the Superfans in *SNL*.

"Da Bears..."

Guy even had the Chicago accent.

Every time he spoke she wondered why she and everyone else she knew didn't have Chicago accents too.

Was this due to the world being more globalized?

Had Chicago become such a big city that people from all regions flooded in and destroyed their drawls?

Gentrification was something that she constantly wondered about and this seemed like a thing she could blame on people who go to Urban Outfitters, and guys with deep obsessions of David Foster Wallace.

Where the fuck did that guy come from?

Like not regionally...

Just in the history of society and, more importantly, literariness.

Fuck was that even a real word?

Fuck it...it didn't matter.

While wondering this she yawned deeply. She wasn't tired but anxious.

Some people play with their hair and tap their hands.

She yawned.

Somewhere she read that yawning increases oxygen flow to the brain and this relieved stress.

She didn't yawn in response to this.

Sometimes a person does something and later finds out that there is a perfectly reasonable reason for it.

Perhaps with research, we can all find out whatever happened to the Chicago accent.

Every time she yawned though people would say things like:

"Nooo, can't be tired."

"Sleep when you're dead."

"Stay up."

"Beat that tired monster into hell."

"Don't yawn...you're making me feel tired."

You know...annoying bullshit that there was no decent response too...

Her go-to reaction would always be to say,"ughhh sorry haven't had my coffee yet."

Guy behind the counter said something along the lines of, "But that's so bad.... coffee can't fix everything."

Bet???

It wasn't just something she used to fix everything. It was also her excuse for most things.

Kind of like how people say things like:

"Sorry about last night. I was just too drunk."

But she was baited and went further into this discussion on her lifestyle choice of needing coffee for everything.

Not that it goddamn mattered but what in this life did?

"You don't drink coffee?"

He responded, "Nah never did. It doesn't work on me. Just makes me more tired..."

Her internet friend said this about his allergy to coffee.

This left her dumbstruck but accepting.

"Well damn. Maybe your're allergic to coffee."

"Nah, it just doesn't work on me."

Whatever, dude. She gave him an out.

She brought her cup back to her seat and watched *Mad Men*.

Later at night she went home and wondered if she would message On-line Guy that she met one of his people, but that's weird and she wasn't that into it in the first place.

Messaging someone something short means them responding with something long.

She hated when that shit happened.

Another day ended and maybe another one would soon begin for Zoe.

Seriously, it was four AM when she got home.

Guess the day began without her.

Too Rad For You

After getting used to teaching, her fear about not becoming a famous writer had left her mind entirely. Now the only thing she spoke about was the Russian Revolution, Gender and Labor Reform, and sometimes politics. It was like she was finally growing up. She went about trying to look busy when she got to her office on campus. She shuffled papers from one side of the desk to the other and shuffled tabs on her trashy desktop, where she hid Facebook and Twitter in the background. Jack, the head of the history department, called her over for their weekly department meetings where they discussed progress and curriculum. Jack very much liked watching Gary Vaynerchuk videos on YouTube, and he took Vaynerchuk's approach to almost everything. When he insisted that they all hustle and never quit, Zoe's mind drifted.

"I don't know what the fuck to do," Zoe thought after the meeting. She didn't feel like working and the complacent feeling she always feared crept into her mind. Suddenly Zoe hated her job. It wasn't the actual teaching or the subject. She hated deadlines and meetings and needing approval before she made any kind of changes to her lectures.

But that was just what working at a college was like. You always had the administration breathing down your back and you never really knew who was in charge. It was like *The Trial* by Franz Kafka but for some deranged reason she wasn't allowed to die in the end.

Zoe went to her office and saved her files on Dropbox, closed Microsoft Word, and messaged Radley.

"Hey!"

"What's up, Zo?"

"Do you want to watch a movie or something?"

"No, Zoe. This isn't Mad Men. I'm not allowed to just leave work in the middle of the day and go to a movie."

"I thought they didn't care about that kind of thing at startups. So, is that a definite 'no'?"

"Pretty much. Look, message me after work. I'll see you at the party." Radley signed off.

Ever since he started working a job he had become so serious.

Zoe walked around campus for a while and then grabbed an Uber to the Music Box Theatre and watched *Harry Potter and the Deathly Hallows Part 1*. She'd seen it in on an Imax screen at Navy Pier years ago with Tyler. They sat right in the middle, hoping to feel more surrounded by magic. She remembered feeling like it was a waste of money. She legit couldn't notice the difference between movies screened in Imax and ones that weren't. They just seemed to be louder.

This theatre was much better and less disorienting. She also preferred going to smaller theatres in general after that one shooting. After an hour in the theatre, she suddenly felt guilty. Radley changed who he was to be here, and she couldn't stay still long enough to be at work for a full day.

Zoe meekly thought to herself, "This is a waste of time and money."

Then she thought, "Life is a waste of time and money."

She pulled out her iPhone and typed "life is a waste of time and money" on her notes app. She felt a little better but she was still depressed. She then took an Uber back to work where she would then spend two and a half hours scrolling through Facebook.

When she finally was done for the day, she got an Uber back apartment just to change her shirt and then headed over to the party.

To give full context, this wasn't a normal party. It was a party thrown by a writer friend.

At the party there were a lot of people that were like nineteen years old. Half of them had already art shows of their own and were talking about how well attended they were. A lot of them did glitter art or wrote woke statements and put them string banners. Others were in DIY bands, wrote novels, or did Miranda July-like performance art.

Zoe hung back and waited for Radley to get there. When he did she was totally embarrassed. He'd come straight from work and wasn't dressed for this kind of party at all. She bought drinks for the two of them and then they hung in corner by the only other person they knew who was around their age: Joe.

They drank PBR and talked about how boring their day jobs were. Really. They were just trying to shut out the sound of sanguinity they were overhearing in some of the conversations that the nineteen-year-olds were having. Zoe sadly noticed that a few of those nineteen-year-olds were in her classes. She avoided eye contact with all of them and was then determined to find more people her age to be around. She didn't understand why these nineteen-year-olds were so optimistic anyways. Only people with money can afford to be in the art world and be optimistic at the same time. Otherwise, they were fucked. To a certain extent, Zoe was fucked from the beginning. Each generation had a group of people that were fucked from the beginning but so far, her generation was the only generation that was fucked entirely. Zoe followed Joe into the house for more be and they both just sort of wallowed in their fuck-edness.

"Check this one out." Joe said.

"What is it?" Zoe said.

"It's some German beer that's like 16% alcohol."

"Lit. Let's drink it."

They drank the beer.

"That's pretty good," Joe said.

"Yeah. I like beer," Zoe shrugged.

"What happened to us?" Joe asked.

"Everyone got younger," Zoe said.

"Isn't that what that one dude said in Dazed and Confused?" Joe asked.

"I don't know. Probably," Zoe saw across the room that Radley was visibly bored.

She walked into another room to avoid the sad and distant look in his eyes and found a bulldog on a couch. It was the perfect place to hide, and the dog didn't seem to mind being pet. They continued to drink and talk about how fucked they were. Joe suggested that Zoe start up a Riot Grrrl band. Zoe suggested that Joe just start making movies of his own instead of waiting to be discovered.

"It's depressing to think about time. Like, if you're in your twenties, eight years is a cool amount of time. You go from twenty to twenty-eight, you still are in your twenties trying to figure stuff out. You can still stay up late and have pizza parties and its kind of cool and existential. After that, eight years is frightening," Zoe said.

Joe hit back, "You think so? I thought thirty was the new twenty."

"I don't know. It's all dumb, I guess. Listen, I'm gonna grab Radley and get out of here. He doesn't seem into this."

In the other room a short writer from Brooklyn was talking about Hegel. He was funny and looked cute. He was popular in some circles and looked like he was going to make it as a legit writer. A bunch of the younger girls stood around listening to him in awe, while pretending to enjoy beer.

Zoe made eye contact with him and quickly drank her beer, grabbed two more and walked outside to hang near the garage of house.

He stopped talking about Hegel and followed. Three people were already hanging there smoking weed and offered some to them. Zoe said she couldn't because they did drug tests at her work. He laughed and asked if she wanted a regular cigarette instead. He pulled out a pack of Marlboros.

It had started raining lightly. Zoe stood next to him smiling and said she only smoked Natural American Spirits. He put away his cigarettes and left.

It was weird.

She stood there in the rain and immediately realized how fucked the whole day was. She basically was just flirting with another dude after saying she was going to look for her own boyfriend because he looked sad. What's worse was that she failed hard at it. Her mind was chaotic. She pulled her phone out of her pocket and just looked at her apps for no reason.

Really, she was just buying time before she had to go back into the party to find Radley and go home.

After a good ten minutes, she looked up and the cute Brooklyn guy was walking towards her with a pack of Natural American Spirits.

"Hey," Zoe tried to say casually.

He smiled and looked at her.

"I wasn't sure which ones you liked so I got the black ones. I saw David Lynch smoke those during the behind the scenes of Twin Peaks and just kind of assumed you'd like them."

She realized he was looking her over far more than she originally thought. His eyes gestured towards her Twin Peaks tattoo on her wrist and the two of them smiled and smoked their cigarettes in the rain.

Radley eventually came out to find her and without a word they looked at each other and knew their relationship was over.

He wasn't angry or sad. He didn't have to socialize in groups that he didn't get anymore. He could go back to Iowa and be the adventurous guy again and not feel bad about not being there for her.

Radley was free to take off his tie and go his own way.

He said she could keep the apartment and that he'd pay through the end of the lease.

Should I Kill Myself or Have a Cup of Coffee?

Zoe started the day off with coffee and Xanax. Both cancelled each other out, but she couldn't really tell.

She messaged Friend A (Tyler) from the suburbs and told him that she wanted to go to Starbucks in his area.

He asked when they should meet and she said, "how about 30 minutes" and he was like, "how about an hour I need so shower."

She said "k" because she also needed to shower and now, she was going to get the opportunity to.

When she ran into the bathroom, she decided that a shower would take way too much time so she dipped her head under the bathtub faucet and rinsed her hair with conditioner instead and then quickly blow dried it. It looked better than before but not that great either.

She threw on her "boyfriend t-shirt" and American Apparel hoodie and headed out. In the elevator going down to her garage she pulled up Spotify on her phone and started to decide what kind of music she was going to listen to on the way to the burbs.

She picked Iron and Wine's cover of "Such Great Heights" because it made her think of her new crush and that made her happy.

She plugged it into the aux cable of her car and hit the road as they say.

30 minutes of smooth driving with minimal traffic and she was at the Starbucks that they always went to. Friend A used to meet her there because she used to live by it. Now he lived by it and she went there to meet him.

At this point I must point out that Friend A is not her crush. Just a friend. But that mistake happens often and that's okay. He liked her for her. Her crush only liked her as an idea. Not a person. Maybe even just an art form left stagnant and waiting.

She thought of a quote that might've been from Trotsky:

"Art, it is said, is not a mirror, but a hammer: it does not reflect, it shapes."

This meant both meant something and nothing to her. She just didn't know what. At this point she messaged Tyler from her car that she was at the Starbucks, since she had no intention of going in there alone to find a seat, but she did so anyways. It was cold out and she didn't want to keep her car running.

The store was crowded full of people working and people with kids. She forgot that it was a weekend.

The only seat left for her was at the counter by the pick-up area. She sat there and mobile ordered a chai latte with a shot of espresso.

He messaged her that he was heading in and asked where she was. She told him but as she was finishing the message a couple came and took the took seats next to her. He hugged her and frowned with disappointment because now there was nowhere for them to sit.

Friend A said "das okay" in a perky voice that he would use if he sensed she was in the middle of a depressive episode. She'd suffered from some serious sadness the night before. She messaged him kind of suicidal things but not totally suicidal since she had gotten over it quickly. She had even forgotten about it until that moment when she heard it in his voice, but she was going to stay in a good mood today because she couldn't have another day like yesterday.

Remembering the night before she also recalled them having a conversation about records and sad hipster playlists and him needing more song suggestions.

They looked for a place to sit and found a crappy two-seat table by a very sunny window. They'd both have to wear sunglasses inside.

Life was crazy.

He ordered a Starbucks reserves coffee, but she couldn't really recall the name. It came from Zimbabwe or somewhere like that. She never understood why he bothered. It cost more than Pike and he ruined the taste by pouring tons of cream and sugar in. It was a waste. But then again, so was life.

She tried to remember which coffee he got so she could ask about it when he sat down.

Before he sat down, he heard that her chai was ready. So he went back and grabbed that too.

She looked at Spotify on her phone so she could find songs for his sad hipster playlist. She selected Iron and Wine's cover of "Such Great Heights" because it just kind of sounded right for a sad hipster playlist and he sat down with their coffee.

She sipped on her chai and thought about her crush and how sometimes crushes are supposed to be just that.

Fugazi Plays to His Insanity in Hospital Waiting Rooms

Tyler was not depressed...just disappointed.

He didn't mind the nurse wondering how he got there. But he did mind living the listless existence he had sadly grown accustomed to. Everyone abandoning him and absolutely nothing in his life working out. He was finally starting to see what it felt like to be a Friend A to a person who would only ever consider him just a friend. Tyler would sit at home alone with notes on his mirror to remind himself to be happy and then go to work with an overly demanding boss. There was nothing to be happy about. Except for his weekends as Friend A. He fulfilled all duties of a boyfriend for Zoe. They went to concerts. They grabbed dinner. He listened to her when her life was a mess. And then time and time again, he'd find her abandoning him. It was like he was some useless minion there to prop her up. She would call him from across the country and then they'd watch MTV together. It was like *When Harry Met Sally*.

But Zoe did not believe in heteronormativity. She believed that guys and girls could be just friends. She hated on that movie several times to him and said it was so problematic in today's world. She said that about a lot of things like the TV series *Friends* or *Sex and the City*. He somewhat got it but also didn't care. He'd just nod in agreement because it made her happy. That's what a friend would do he thought.

So that's what Tyler was. Friend A. A for asexual. That's what he told her. She loved that because she was bisexual and just didn't know many other people in the Alphabet Squad who weren't just gay or lesbian. So when he said he was an Ace, she was psyched. Until her boyfriend from Iowa came home to stay. Then Tyler said he was aromantic, and that he needed more and stopped talking to her for two weeks. For those two weeks she spent time talking to her therapist trying to better understand his feelings and exactly what he wanted out of a friendship. Neither of them felt woke enough to get what aromantic exactly meant or if he was just throwing the word around.

He got used to the boyfriend, and then the boyfriend left because Zoe found someone else. Someone that fit more. Tyler hated that she never attempted to make him fit at all or see that they did. But the sad truth of it was that he had taken advantage of her trust by being whatever she needed him to be until it was his chance. He never wanted to be Friend A.

Earlier that day he was getting coffee. Now he was sitting in a waiting room, guarded by nurses who took away his cellphones, headphones, and shoelaces.

The silence irritated him so he head-banged to the only music he could remember in his mind while his parents who didn't know what to do with him talked to the doctors.

He sat and recalled his life in the suburbs, which led him to corporate-structured Apple stores with big lines and small products. And it was there that he discovered that we sell souls to mask our mass perceptions. Instead of learning to spell the words to hear them out we built white knuckled deities into blood shot evenings, forming giants in our midst.

Any form of material possession to make the dark thoughts go away was worth it. No matter how much it cost. For the first few days of buying something new you get an adrenaline rush and people's attention.

But that was no longer enough.

Tyler had holstered his glazed goodbye to the world colliding. His truths coming out.

He tried to go down lanes and not across streets, while listening to Daughter in his apartment earlier that day. Petty remorse echoed in his hollowed-out bedroom. He imagined the looks on his mother's face when she would see her last-born die first, but heard words echo out that mortality was not a watch tied to bound hands.

He was forced to go to a doctor's office that smelled like damp paint but was given reprieve by the doctor who said he would see Tyler next week with a recommendation for a good psychiatrist who could spend more time analyzing him to reach a proper diagnosis. For now, he should stay at his parents' house.

He wasn't depressed. He was disappointed.

Reasons For Zoe's Relationships in Direct Correlation With Her Age:

14. Everyone else was doing it and she didn't want to be left out. Boy seemed cute enough and their "meet-cute" was simply adorable. Too bad they really couldn't stand each other; she could have made a name for herself writing a love story about them. In a film, boy would probably be played by Michael Cera.

16. Her best friend liked him. Zoe wanted to prove she wasn't too dorky to be datable, so she stole him before best friend could even make a move. She was pissed. Too bad Zoe really wasn't ready to date still. Zoe's mom would later tell her she was a late bloomer. Maybe she was right. Zoe heard guy was married now. Wild.

17. Their friend hooked them up. She wasn't really attracted to the guy and she didn't think he was really attracted to her. Thank god they didn't last long and became decent friends. She thought he might be gay anyhow. She didn't judge...but she was wrong. He was engaged now to a girl that Zoe met once.

18. Boy had an undeniable charisma. He owned the Kurt Shirt. She didn't want to go to college without the fabled "summer fling". He was it. Their relationship ended as quickly as it started. She still didn't really "get" him.

18. He was raffish and smart. They met in philosophy class. It seemed like a good idea at the time. He said she seemed like a player. She didn't know a girl could be considered one. That guy was sort of right...

18. She was lonely and didn't fit in at school. He would visit her every chance he got, and it made her feel loved. She was sorry she didn't love him back.

19. It was her first time having sex and she fell in love. That's what she thought you did after you had sex. Girl corrected Zoe's foolishness. She wouldn't make that mistake again. But she still couldn't listen to Tegan and Sara without thinking about her.

19. Zoe was lovesick from her prior escapade. He comforted her and She guessed she wanted to just know if she was the same person as she was before--back when they had their summer fling. She wasn't. It's a shame; he never did get over her. She wished he would.

21. Girl preyed upon Zoe's love for all the wrong reasons and made her fall in love sort of. Now Zoe thought she was just in a bad place emotionally and that Girl was in the right place in the right time. Or Zoe was in the wrong place at the wrong time. They were bad together and she kept telling herself she'd break up with Girl. It took a while...

21. He was the person she'd whisper to at parties and text when she was bored. He brought her adventure and love. They stayed together until she moved to San Francisco.

28. She really had no idea. She met him at a poetry reading and they hit it off. They were both obsessed with Russian history and literature. They probably could've stayed together longer but for some weird reason they started to disagree politically. He was an anarchist. She was a communist. It didn't matter. Zoe was leaving that city anyways.

30. He was in a car with her for 36 hours straight and made her laugh and smile the entire time. They lived in different states but decided to try and make it work. It eventually didn't. But, wildly enough, neither of them were too upset about it. They just wanted each other to be happy. Zoe felt that was probably what legit love probably was.

The Lost Art of Not Trying

Xanax and coffee always had a weird mix. It almost always felt like a hopeless and useless combination.

Like Zoe wondered if the punch of the Xanax would ever be enough to really undo the caffeine.

But in the end, it sort of did and sort of didn't. Like instead of a mellow hit on the brakes, it was a sudden feeling of everything is going to be alright.

You got a very chill and relaxed feeling of productivity. She needed that with her current job. Grading essays and doing research of her own. She spent forever learning of Russian history and was now determined to learn more about socialism in Chicago.

She felt that mellow feeling at that exact moment. She was on a shitty couch she bought off Amazon in her apartment in Wicker Park with Portlandia, but had it paused on the TV in front of her.

She already decided she wasn't going to watch it but getting off the couch to turn it off felt kind of pointless for the moment. Instead, all she wanted to do is write and document stuff for at least a little bit.

She decided that her mom's mind was probably slipping because she didn't take diaries and that she'd lived so long and had so many kids that it was probably easy for her to lose track of things and kids and narratives of the children's lives.

That all made a lot of sense, but she really focused more on the fact that her parents didn't remember anything about her.

Every single time Zoe asked her dad what he said to other people about her he responded with how she was his "most cost-effective child."

Humiliating.

It made her feel like all she was nothing but a dollar sign, and the plus side was that her dollar sign was somehow smaller than brother's and sister's.

What was worse was that he didn't even equate the fact that her college education was cheap because she dropped out and then finished on her own dime. She couldn't stand the career they wanted for her and if she wanted to study her thing, she'd have to do it on her own.

Even her siblings remembered that enough to still make fun of her.

She secretly got her PhD without telling any of them and was a professor now. Zoe didn't tell any of them because she knew they'd ruin the good feeling.

For some reason she kind of thought that her parents would be proud of her but one day they started talking about how she was wasting her life writing. It wasn't worth giving them the satisfaction of telling them she got a real job.

She even knew that real job was still not going to be real enough for them. Anything that didn't have to do with law or business they didn't care about. She would never be the person they wanted her to be.

For that reason, she would never be a child that they genuinely loved. Her mom tried to make up for that by doing small things like giving Zoe pills that she needed or running errands for her.

At that exact moment Zoe's mom texted her and asked what happened with Tyler. Zoe was nervous and had no idea. But she was shocked to see that her mom remembered her friend's name and paid attention to what was happening in his life.

Apparently, he'd had a breakdown. Zoe wished there were something she could do.

What is to Be Done?

There was an insane fire in California happening, and she was sitting in the West Loop of Chicago in the cold.

Chicago be lame like that.

She'd had Chai earlier but began jonesing for another coffee.

She couldn't decide whether she was going to wait till after 4:30 for coffee or go for it and just get it then.

Who knows which we she went on that one.

What we all know is that she would drink decaf when she got home later. Maybe grab some tacos too.

Girl must get a bit of a reward after waking up on a day like that one, right?

She was having a weird Carrie Bradshaw moment and was thinking of watching *Sex and the City* later. Every aspect of that show was making her think of the history class she was teaching at the time.

One book she listed for the required reading was straight up called *Sex and the City*.

It sounded sassy but wasn't. It was just about whores and London in the 19th century.

I mean sassy. Maybe for its time?

idk

The whole Carrie Bradshaw moment she was having was also because of her other history course she was teaching about Gender and Jamestown.

They discussed diaries and how they were not always reliable sources.

Lots of dude wrote bullshit diaries back then and they overinflated their sexuality and masculinity and other shit because they felt that their patriarchy was threatened?

Little did they know was that shit wouldn't be legit threatened until the 21st century.

Anyhow, she was wondering what kind of things Carrie Bradshaw would be bullshitting about on the show if she were a real person. Was she trying to veil her insecurities in some sham feminine way to appear demurer or feminine?

Did she like shoes or was she playing to this idea that to be a woman was to be flaky and full of material obsession?

There Zoe fucking went again...

Communism.

The Drug Dealer's Apartment Decorated with Kafka, David Foster Wallace, Bukowski, and Metallica

Zoe and Evan sat around in Billie's apartment. Billie smoking weed while grabbing a box of Xanax for Zoe.

"So, what's up bitches?" Billie asked while rummaging around her apartment.

"We were a warehouse party with Elle. What happened? Why didn't you go?" Evan asked.

"I had a late night of work and couldn't make it, "Zoe lied. Actually, she had binge-watched Netflix and used the last of her Xanax to hype herself up for the party. The less anxiety she had, the more fun she was to be around. Sadly, it didn't work, and she was now out of Xanax and the pharmacy wouldn't refill her prescription. That's why it was useful to know at least a few shady people.

"Lit. Legit film cameras are king," Evan said as he was looking at Billie's bookshelf while she was rummaging around her apartment for pills. He grabbed the Pentax from the bookshelf to show Zoe.

"Fuck, I think I'm out of Xanax. I have tons of Ativan though. Is that cool? Billie asked.

Zoe collapsed into Billie's beanbag, gazed up at Billie's LED lights on the ceiling, and slowly nodded her head.

Billie handed the Zoe the pills and snatched the Pentax away from Evan. "How was the warehouse thing? Anything wild go down?" Billie asked Evan as she put her camera back on her bookshelf where it belonged.

"Meh. It was just another literary thing. Some people were way too old to still be into that kinda shit and everyone else were like a bunch of Gen Z kids talking about Gen Z shit. Elle and I were probably the only Millennials there," Evan said.

"Elle did score some points with one of the older dudes at least. I was trying to learn how to Renegade, and she was networking." Evan said. "Bruh, can you do it now? Please don't tell me you wasted your time with a fuck ton of gen Z peeps and didn't pick anything up," Billie begged, "I'd like to see you do it. Maybe you should withhold his stuff until her does it," Zoe said to Billie.

"Bet. Hot do it, bruh!" Billie said.

"It was actually really hard." Evan said. "Or I was really drunk. Can't we just listen to some music or watch stuff on YouTube or something?"

Zoe laughed at Evan as he tried to dodge. She was no longer the dork in that room.

"Hold up Ev. You're saying twelve-year-old kids can do this shit and you can't?"

"I think that's exactly what he's saying, Zoe. Dude can't learn a little dance. This is why every generation hates us," Billie took out her Mac-Book and gave it to Evan.

"We'll watch YouTube videos with you if you do the dance, "Billie said to Evan.

She went straight to Spotify on her Mac and turned the song on.

[138]

"It's up to you, Ev. You do it and we'll watch Monty Python or SNL or whatever on here."

Evan got up and gave it his best shot and then fell backwards.

"Yeah, I don't think that's how that dance goes," laughed Zoe.

"That was pretty cringe," Billie chimed in while laughing.

"Fuck you. At least I tried. The only thing you two do is learn their slang and nothing else," Evan fired back.

Zoe popped a pill. Billie turned off Spotify and pulled up some SNL skits on YouTube.

Evan flipped through videos and finally found one that he liked: Matt Foley, Motivational Speaker.

Billie air played it onto the TV so they could all watch.

"SNL just isn't that great anymore," Zoe said, "Portlandia is way better."

"Ugh that hipster show? You would..."

"What? Carrie Brownstein is icon. Hot too."

Evan was annoyed at Billie and Zoe talking through the skit.

"Okay. SNL isn't that hot anymore. Can we please just watch?" Evan restarted the skit.

"Sorry, Ev. It's not a terrible show. It's just not amazing anymore," Billie suggested.

"Actually, it is pretty amazing when political shit happens. I watch every skit when an election is going down," Zoe said as she sunk further into the beanbag.

They watched a whole hour of "classic" SNL skits from the 90's and then Billie disappeared into her bedroom for a hot minute and came back.

"Yo, try this shit," Billie said as she did a line of coke.

Evan took a bump and handed it to Zoe. She was undecided, thinking she might have a panic attack or that her work might do a drug test. "Nah, I'm good. Besides, I just had Xanax. I think that combination would just cancel that out."

As they got fucked up, Zoe pulled out her phone and tried to think of something clever to tweet. All she ever wanted to tweet was that "life is a waste of time and money" or something like that. She never did because she knew she'd get weird messages from followers or friends. Instead, she just took a picture of Billie's cool LED lights.

She just didn't get why her generation was just so fucked up. Not fucked up in the way that Baby Boomers had fucked them. But fucked up in the way that they could never truly "adult" or adapt to things without drugs. She slowly pretended to give a fuck about the time on her watch and said, "Fuck, I have a ton of work to get done. Guess I gotta go."

She pulled herself up from the beanbag. She wasn't judging them. She just didn't get it and she wanted to just be in bed. For some reason it felt better to feel "tiny and alone" there than it was to feel "tiny and alone" anywhere else.

Life really was just a waste of time and money.

The Graduate

Towards the end of the fall semester of classes was Hanukah.

She rode the train each day to classes and this constantly led to new and weird experiences.

As a would-be writer, this situation made her life even better but as a new professor this sucked. So much time wasted.

She would constantly have to wake up early and make shitty breakfast and shitty coffee and put it in a crappy thermos, and then lug it all onto a train that was typically so crowded that she couldn't even move.

She finally got the hint that she should start dressing a bit more professional at work when a student hit her up for Adderall, so she was starting to do that bullshit too.

Now, she looked like an adult.

FUCK.

Like before she would roam the hallways and kids didn't even notice it because she was short as hell and young looking.

She was so fucking lucky.

Now she stuck out as the superior and that sucked.

She only thought about this because it meant that she had to start wearing nice adult shoes, which also made her commute hell.

On the train, she sipped her coffee to feel better but 'lord fucking fire' it was hot.

She couldn't spit it out or make an ACKKK sound so instantly she just had to feel the burn inside her heart and mind and never sipped from it again.

As she was getting off at the Jackson stop, she waited in line on the escalator to go to the street level.

A homeless guy...or a crappy hipster...turned back and asked, "Is your name Rachel? You look like a Jew...Your name is for sure Rachel, right?"

She just averted eye contact and had no idea how to respond so didn't. Her headphones were in, so it was something she could sort of ignore.

It was odd as fuck though. Someone at work the day before said "Hope you have a good Hanukkah..."

When she got into the classroom she finally began to wonder whether she had Jewish ancestry. How could someone even determine such a thing just by looking at her outward appearance? It all seemed racist and wrong.

Her parents didn't know, and she didn't want to contact her birth parents, so she decided she should take one of those "23 and me" tests.

Her brother and sister scolded her that those kinds of tests were the government's way of collecting your DNA.

Honestly it really could be, but wtf were they honestly going to do with it?

Clone her?

They weren't gonna clone a five-foot tall, panicky, bipolar, maybe-Jewish girl with a history with walking into things.

Might as well live dangerously and do it.

The whole thing sounded fun until she got the test and realized how much she would have to spit in a cup to get the results.

From Wicker Park to Hell

"Ihop coffee sucks," she thought while still bitterly drinking it.

The coffee came with ten creamers and like a million sugars. She used about half of that and intended to the use the rest once there was enough room in the cup to fill it.

She originally was going to go out for brunch and coffee with a friend but she woke up depressed again and later than when she and her friend had originally decided.

Really, she set herself up for failure.

The plan was to wake up at five AM.

Five fucking AM.

But she was awake till three AM trying to force herself to sleep while also considering spending the rest of her night on the balcony listening to music.

She knew that either last night or tonight there was supposed to be a neighbor's party, but she just couldn't remember. At least they were polite enough to tell other people in the building so no one would get pissed off.

When she lived in Roscoe Village, neighbors threw a Fourth of July party on their roof and blasted Bruce Springsteen and fireworks the entire night. She wouldn't have minded the first two things and found the fireworks awesome, if it weren't for the fact that the neighbor invited a lot of people with kids to that party and they were loud as hell. Even louder than the fireworks and Bruce Springsteen.

She compromised with herself at three AM that night and took a Xanax and listened to music in her bedroom with her cat in bed.

The morning came and she ordered the coffee off DoorDash.

Postmates pissed her off two days before and she swore never to use them again.

The funny thing is that she knew she would use it again but not soon enough for her to be so aware of how annoying they were.

It was Saturday. Bastille Day. She was on a couch drinking bad coffee in Chicago. At least she had coffee and was watching *The Handmaid's Tale* again.

Last episode of season two. That episode was mad crazy. Anyone who saw it could agree on that.

Like, seriously, how were they going to move on with the story now?

She got brunch with her friend the next day and annoyed him the entire time about it.

It is what it is

It'd been a long time since Zoe has actually read or written or done anything not school related. Coffee no longer gave her the edge to do anything after work. So, at the end of each day, she just passed out and hoped the weekend would come soon.

She was teaching cool classes that semester but in one of the classes she taught with another professor. She needed to trade twitter handles with him and he laughed about her bio area on her Twitter, and he was like "That's morbid but funny", and she was like, "Dude, that's a quote from Albert Camus. We're professors. How did you not get that..."and he was like "Wtf? From which book?" and she was like, "Nah, not from a book... just a quote...something he said..." and the other professor kept asking which book in an annoying way to prove her wrong, she thought. She embarrassed him for not knowing the quote and he was determined to prove she was full of shit.

Life sucked sometimes.

Coffee was better.

She had to drink coffee on the regular and the other professor consistently made fun of her about it.

She was always out of money and he kept asking why didn't she save cash and buy less.

She said, "For sure", but still got four-dollar cold Starbucks bottle drinks from the vending machine every Tuesday.

Her busy day. When she taught with him.

Fuck Tuesdays.

The other professor was so damn weird and all up in her business all the time. But he did do her a solid and showed her an area in the school that had an actual Starbucks so she wouldn't have to drink the stuff from the vending machine.

Good on him.

She asked whether it was like a regular Starbucks or one of those weird small ones that only serve Pike Place.

Professor idgaf was like, "yeah but it's not as good."

The next class she taught with him he had Dunkin Donuts coffee.

Dick couldn't talk about coffee when he drank that. Only losers drank DD according to Zoe.

Like how the hell did he talk shit about Starbucks when he drank basically cardboard-tasting coffee.

She lost what little respect she had for him and got the second floor Starbucks.

It was still better than the vending machine coffee and way better than DD.

PS... other professor guy kept offering her to drink his DD coffee...wtf?

Mood: Ted Bundy Representing Himself at His Own Trial

The day after her terrible hangover she decided that she finally needed coffee.

She woke up feeling slightly energetic but knew that this was a fleeting feeling so she immediately went to the Postmates app on her phone to order coffee.

After looking for a minute or two, she realized she had deleted it the week before in an effort to save money and possibly lose weight.

Today was not the day to save money or lose weight though.

She downloaded it again, hoping that it still had her credit card information so she wouldn't have to walk into the closet with her backpack and credit card.

She decided that she might as well order breakfast on the app as well to avoid the small bag fee.

After ordering, she felt regret and happiness at the same time.

Fuck life was sad.

She looked at the app and saw that it was already too late to cancel the order. So she leaned into it and held onto the positive feeling.

Now she wouldn't have to go grind the Stumptown coffee beans and put the grounds into the coffee machine and wait for them to brew.

Now she could just hang on the couch watching that Ted Bundy thing on Netflix and chill.

She never wanted anyone to know she was this lazy and sad, so she strategically posted random social media pics with the illusion that she was actually out or she was home from an early workday.

Everyone probably did this.

She took a picture of the coffee she got and wrote the caption "after work-out reward."

Lying fuck.

She smiled, knowing that people probably believed it and maybe even felt a little bit bad about their own laziness.

Mission accomplished.

She then watched two hours of Ted Bundy and in two months, she'd actually have to go back to work at some point.

Just not then.

Transmissions from the City Heart

Zoe sat at her desk on the first floor of the archive library drinking a Venti Iced Caramel Macchiato and wondered how the fuck anyone knew how to spell macchiato. Thankfully, she had Grammarly on her web app and had it autocorrect. She did this with almost any word she didn't know how to spell. It was a sad thing to admit really.

She was thrown into advanced classes so early on in life that she never learned the basics. She always said that this was because she showed such promise early on, but she never really knew if this was the case or if her teachers just assumed she would be just as smart as her older brother. Will always seemed to excel at things that she could not. He was bright-eyed and friendly, and she was dark and silent. Not dark in an ominous way but in her complexion and eyes. You could put the two of them together and never guess that they were related. And that would be correct. They weren't. She was adopted after her parent's lost a baby in childbirth. But yes, he was tall and confident, and she had a personality that fit her small frame.

When she was in first grade a friend picked on her by teasing that she was so short that she looked like a kindergartener. She internalized it immediately because she already knew it to be true. Everyone assured her that looking younger was a good thing and that she'd be grateful when she was thirty to look twenty. Sadly, that myth was such bullshit that would rather just not think about anymore. She was thirty and did not look twenty. She just acted twenty. She felt she aged rapidly due to stress and depression. That her looks dwindled with each tired thought and wide-eyed night that she spent wondering when she was going to die and whether it was going to hurt.

Everyone dies she would think in bed staring at her ceiling.

Everyone also hurts.

But that had nothing to do with why Zoe didn't know how to spell well or why grammar skills were limited to guesswork and sounding it out. Simple tricks constantly ran through her mind: "i before e" and whatnot.

Will knew how to spell. Then again, Will was always better than she was.

As she finished her coffee and headed back up to the archive to look at preserved copies of Left Front Magazine for a new thesis she was working on, she got stopped by security and was told that interns worked downstairs. She showed her badge and he laughed. According to him, she looked twenty-three.

I guess sometimes you just feel old on the inside...

Pill Hill

Zoe spent her day really checking out Chicago. She'd lived there most of her life but never really left the Northside. That Day she decided to check out Calumet Heights. There was a neighborhood there called Pill Hill. It was originally settled by farmers, but the demographic changed during the Black Migration. She wondered if that had anything to do with the nickname for the neighborhood. The dwindling resources and crumbling infrastructure gave her that vibe. But no. Apparently, it was named that after a playwright named Sam Kelley wrote a play called *Pill Hill* and had it set in that neighborhood. She set out to find any kind of coffee shop in the area.

The closest one she found was called South Shore Brew and it was pretty lit. Hipstery though. This concerned her because she knew once those coffee shops sprung up, gentrification was soon to come. She witnessed this in Wicker Park and then Logan Square. People were trying to do it in Pilsen and Humboldt Park and were sort of succeeding. In Pilsen more than Humboldt Park. There were still some areas a person shouldn't go. But then again, it did play host to Riot Fest one year and that musical festival was white as hell. She heard once that a guy every now and then fired a gun in the air for no reason other than to scare white people from moving nearby so rent prices would stay down. She found this brilliant. But there weren't enough gunshots in the world to keep white people from going to coffee shops and music festivals. Especially if those music festivals hosted almost only emo bands.

When she got home at eight PM she finally went out to go get the beer she had been promising her friend all day. She almost didn't go because she got bogged down by rain and depression but still went.

But her therapist confirmed it a week later. She was seriously depressed. It's one thing to say it and another to hear someone else confirm it.

Fuck.

She took the elevator down to the lobby of her building and quickly reminded herself of her growing problems with anxiety. She hadn't exactly had a panic attack in a while, but she had felt the feeling that she would panic for two weeks. Because of this she had been on Xanax nonstop for those two weeks.

She grew more and more fearful of a possible addiction and had promising herself that she'd go the day without it. Then again, she had promised herself that for the last week and it didn't happen but whatever.

The next day, on her way to Starbucks she finally admitted that coffee wasn't something she should really get if it was going to cause her to just need Xanax later. But she still wanted to go out because depression.

It was funny to have to choose between the two. She decided that she'd try to not feel both, so she compromised and got comfort and wellness tea and worked on her writing. Things were going kind of alright for her.

Coffee, Coffee, Coffeeee

There were way too many coffee days and dates that she went to but could no longer remember. She was at a Starbucks in Oldtown wondering what days she might've missed and how it was so strange that her life had become so foggy.

It had been actual months since she'd last seen her therapist and even longer since she'd seen her psych. They say the hardest thing about being mentally ill is sticking to a routine. That routine had officially gone to hell. Now she stayed up all night getting drinks with friends and all-day chugging coffee and watching Netflix or getting sushi or something else.

I think she was trying to remember her coffee hangout with her friend Kristen. They started in Garfield park and ended up on the edge of Wicker Park.

When pulling up to the great coffee place that Kristen insisted that she had to see Zoe saw a hot guy walking across the street.

She insisted that he looked like the guy from the hangover, but Zoe immediately recognized him as a writer that she met in Miami. Or at least she thought it was him...

She knew he had recently moved to Chicago for a bit, but she had no idea of knowing or not knowing whether it was him.

Sure, she could've messaged the dude and be like "is this you," but if it wasn't then that would be awkward and weird, and she'd made a point in life of trying to minimize those awkward and weird moments.

They had a cigarette in Kristen's car for a bit and then grabbed the coffee. The place was called Tempesta Market and it immediately made her think of the original Starbucks store at Pike Place market. The girl at the counter was cute and Zoe was pretty sure that the barista was flirting. But she also might've been gunning for a tip. Little did barista know, she wasn't paying. It was Kristen's turn, and she was cheap.

Poor barista, flirted with the wrong person.

But oh well, that's the way the cookie crumbles.

Oh yeah, Zoe also got a cookie...

Unapolegetically You

"at least you look fuckable hot today" guy off Tinder messaged her a few minutes ago.

She continued to message him on Twitter for another hour even though she felt a tad bad about this.

Like was she not fuckable hot other days? He swiped right so she must be.

Bitch gotta feel good about herself.

This conversation really didn't exist in terms of words after he said that. It legitimately became one hour of gif reactions to each other.

He would message her: Zoe, Stamos dancing with Becky from Full House.

She sent him a gif of that one hot guard in OITNB doing the striptease in the season where they have a riot.

It was on her mind because she was re-binging to prep for the next season that was about to drop.

Anyhow, the point of this gif war was simple:

She wanted coffee and she wanted him to buy it for her.

Like not just go out for it with her.

She wanted to get in his car and pick her up and bring her to the coffee and then buy her said coffee.

She couldn't decide if this was step forward for feminism or not.

Like yeah. It's a dude buying shit for a chick which can seem a bit old-fashioned, but also it was all something she was controlling...like she was busting her ass to have the power in the situation.

She decided that this was totally all right for womanhood, post-Trump.

Girl gotta get her coffee and dude legit must buy it for her.

Maybe it was like payment for years of sexism and unwarranted of dick pics?

Or at least it could compensation for him making her think she wasn't fuckable hot other days.

She was definitely fuckable hot other days...

Sorry I'd Rather Tweet than Write my Novel, but this is the Medium of My Age

A woman is falling off the top of a building. The building is high and you don't know where you are. But you see a window and you realize now that you are inside the building from which she is falling. People gather at the window and stare out with their cellphones in their hands. The woman still falling, tosses and flails about like she a gymnast doing somersaults. She is going to die. You know it. She knows it. The people filming know it. And it can't be stopped it. It can just be known.

There was a test today. You lift your head lazily from your desk and stare blankly around. Everything is familiar. But you don't remember having a test today. And you know you didn't study. You stomach flips as your sweaty palms reach for your pencil and you remember your age. You don't belong here. You already did this. The teacher looks at you like you're crazy when you stand up in angst and then there is a clamor. Everyone rushes to the window. There is a woman in a white blouse falling from on top of the building.

The lobby is large and colorless. The windows stretch from the floor to the ceiling. This makes you think of the World Trade Center as you slowly approach the glass. You look out and remember that the woman is still falling. You wonder how this is possible.

You remember going to school on your birthday and being told that the towers fell and wondering why your parents didn't tell you. Your fifth-grade teacher cried as she stared at the TV on wheels that she brought to the classroom to watch. You remember patriotic songs being played and students being pulled out of class by their parents. One after the other like a revolving door, parents would come and take their kids home. It was a day for family. But your parents never came. Even though it was your birthday. Even though America was under attack. They didn't tell you. And they didn't take you home early. So you watched the TV strapped to the cart on wheels with your teacher and the four other students who also weren't loved by their parents. Every channel played it on loop: towers being hit by planes. You didn't understand but you did remember. You remember people falling out of the buildings hard and fast. You barely saw it. But it happened. There was nothing anyone could do.

But the woman falling off your building was still falling and you're an adult. You're not in school and she is still falling. Her skirt ruffles in the wind and for a second you see her face and hate yourself. She keeps falling and every level she passes you are on. And this fact has not been lost on you. Your eye contact doesn't break, and you know she sees you as you see her fall. You wonder if this is as awkward for her as it is for you. You imagine how embarrassing it must be. To be falling and to have no one help you. But you imagine that she surely must know that there is nothing anyone can do. But you want to do something. But as she hits the ground all you can think to do is to say you're sorry. And you do. To her lifeless corpse. That you are now standing over. Outside of Prudential Plaza in front of Millennium Park. Why does everyone have to die?

Zoe woke up in a cold sweat with her cat next to her. The melatonin she had to take to fall asleep was causing her to have weird and vivid dreams.

The Only Living Girl in Chicago

It was early in the morning and she could no longer say that she was "as real as they come."

Waking up and listening to *Untitled Unmastered* on her iPhone, she walked around the apartment putting on clothes found on the floor.

She drank last night's coffee while thinking that she'd like to travel but then got massive anxiety from the idea of actually having to plan something like that.

She changed her over-ear Bluetooth headphones to her Apple earbuds and the music to Roo Panes since she felt less intense and more detached.

She stepped out of her apartment and her black American Apparel hoodie and iPhone helped hide her from the real world. Maybe they acted like a shroud to protect her from outsiders trying to talk to her or a safety blanket that she just couldn't stop using. A bubble, perhaps, that only she could exist in. It didn't matter. She didn't think about it too much though. She thought of things like poetry and depression more.

We never think about some things yet we focus so intensely on other things. Breathing, for example, is something people don't really think about, but it's something we are constantly doing. We take it for granted. It's funny how when you stop and consider your lungs going up and down the natural rhythm is thrown off.

Her anxiety flared up and she thought she was dying.

I guess that's why people don't think about some things. If we did, we would constantly think we were dying and then be forced to acknowledge the fact that we actually are, and all of this is just time to burn before that happens.

She stopped at the 7-11 on the corner to grab more coffee before work and took a picture of "Bae" and sent it to guy she had sex with last night, with the caption "Sweaty face, he must've been busy last night." Approximately five minutes later, the guy she fucked replied, "LOL."

She and the guy had wandered so late last night that it was almost morning when they got back to her place. Before coming up for sex he needed to stop at at 7-11 for Natural American Spirits and condoms. The Asian shopkeeper hung at the counter while talking to his wife on his iPhone–another man, another bubble.

His name was Jim, but nobody cared. He was "Bae the 7-11 guy". Even his wife called him Bae.

The guy she was fucking laughed with her and they imagined Jim going to sleep each night and waking up each day to his wife saying things like:

"G'morning, Bae."

"I love you, Bae,"

"Fuck me harder, Bae."

"Why don't you buy me nice things for me anymore, Bae."

She stopped texting the guy from last night and walked past the park on the way to work. Some people were in bubbles, other people weren't. A world full of people shielded in opaque kind of watery things is kind of beautiful and just kind of weird like James Cameron's Avatar.

One guy on the sidewalk looked like he was yelling and she typed in her notes app, "The sun is sort of warmish this morning. I thought I would feel refreshed, instead I just feel dazed."

Staring at cracks on the sidewalk, she rushed to the L to get to work. A few dead trees curled over the Blue Line platform and created silhouettes into the blazing light pollution of Wicker Park.

Getting to work seemed to take twice as long that day. She entered her department office, a monolithic structure that made her think of Space Odyssey and think about how she'd probably be there until she'd die or get laid off. Both were likely and thinking of both made her anxious. The college campus had a no tech policy and she hated them for it, but she still took her earbuds out. She began to get a rush of some underlying feeling. She couldn't find a word for it or explain where it existed in her body, but she knew it. The world was a better place outside.

Several hours later, she woke up in the grass in the park by the L with her friends drinking wine and eating donuts around her. She thought of socialism and wondered where her phone was until she found it on top of the Starbucks cup next to her.

"Are you going to sleep forever?" is a note she had written before.

"You think you'll have your job forever?" the guy from last night texted her.

She sent him a picture of a dog in the park with the caption, "Is that like forever in dog years or is it just how bored you are?"

He replied, "Yeah. I guess I have too much time on my hands. We should hang again sometime."

She texted him for a few more minutes before putting her phone down to be still with her friends and stop thinking about people and bubbles and him and whether she should quit her job.

Later, she walked home from the park. The guy from that morning was still yelling to himself so she put her earbuds in.

"If this could only just be an ocean with no noise, no people, no jobs; just an endless progression of water, clouds and maybe a sidewalk to walk over it," she thought.

She listened to bands on Spotify when she got home and read an article about Dogecoin. Afterward, she read part of a dissertation called "Exploring the Psychic Roots of Hikikomori in Japan." The phrase hikikomori, literarily meant to be confined to the inside.

She tried to watch a Russian movie from the 70s, looked at her phone's clock, decided she should watch the movie tomorrow, then she read the first sentence of a Miranda July story, decided she would watch the movie, watched two minutes of the movie, turned it off, and tried to meditate.

She just sat on the floor with her eyes closed and thought (while trying not to think) things like:

"You need to a new job. You should act like a grown up."

"You should move to Portland and be who you've been trying to be here."

"I could probably see myself eventually feeling something there."

[164]

Then she tried to quiet her thoughts and focus on meditation, but it didn't work. She moved to her bed and laid there for an hour.

She was too lazy to run. Too cowardly to move. Too afraid to quit her job.

She turned around and saw a reflection of herself in her TV and said, "Fuck this is all so pointless" and left her building to go for a walk.

Sporadic trees and fire hydrants lined her block. She considered taking an Uber to the 24hr Starbucks to get an espresso or maybe take a Valium instead.

But then all she could envision was going home afterwards and getting no rest on a tear-stained pillow.

The skies blackened and blood like lightning flashed.

Water gave her optimism. A blast of euphoria. Flashes of beauty and hope battled with her heart on that lonely street.

She could choose to self-defenestrate from work tomorrow or she could live.

A stray cat came to her as she sat on the sidewalk on that lonely street as the rain drizzled. The "here and now" feeling came to her and for one hot second, everything was okay.

Never Say Goodbye to Chicago

It was now officially five years after John had died. Her favorite writer. Her favorite poet. Her favorite friend. This was something she would never tell Tyler. Especially now that Tyler was suffering mental health issues of his own.

She never got over how John left her and she was terrified that Tyler might go in a similar way.

She spent the whole night trying to remember what she was doing days before she found out her favorite friend was gone forever five years go:

She remembered she was on a high from doing poetry readings for four days, back-to-back.

"I am a visitor here, I'm not permanent," Zoe kept humming as she walked to a food place on the corner. She ordered a medianoche and colada to split with her boyfriend. They were in Miami. John was going to join them but bailed on the last minute. They were both writers, and she really wanted to have him read a piece they wrote together with her. She didn't know it was their last piece and when he died it killed her to realize that.

As Zoe grabbed the colada, she remembered the other writers there saying, on the first night she was in Miami, that if you were to drink a colada by yourself, it would make your heart literally explode.

Zoe was definitely the kind of person to put this to the test.

When she was at the food place, she assumed the other writers were off somewhere doing coke or something. She was feeling antisocial; this wasn't the first time that she found herself at a lit event to meet people at, where she eventually found herself off exploring on her own with her boyfriend.

She and her boyfriend enjoyed the Miami sun while waiting for the colada and she could tell that he was really living his best life right now and she worried that she never would be. She wasn't really sure what her best life was honestly, and it occurred to her that she should probably be tweeting those thoughts.

She picked up her iPhone X to tweet, but nothing felt of true significance other than "hail satan" or "coffee for life bitches".

Neither of those two things made it onto her account though. Just a pic of the coffee and a unicorn emoji.

But in the background she heard people rushing towards her and laughing, "Whoa! What a crazy coincidence! Hey, guys!"

She looked up and saw the other writers.

It was wild.

Thinking about it all now felt weird and surreal because something similar happened with her and John at their last poetry reading in Portland. It was the last time she ever saw him in person. Instead of medianoches and coffee, they bumped into each other at Voodoo Donuts. It was the last shift of the night. So they were given a bucket of donuts. John joined Zoe and her boyfriend in an alleyway between Voodoo Donuts and a strip club. John said he was totally going to write about it in his novel later while on the plane home. She never knew if he did.

But there in Miami, she was with a different crowd of literary people. When she ditched John back in Portland and bumped into him again, she found out he spent the day checking out bookstores and food trucks. With the Miami writers, she found out they had been kicked out of two nightclubs and still somehow couldn't find coke. Which was weird as hell seeing as how they were in Miami. Zoe and her boyfriend hung with the Miami writers after bumping into them by an old pool with no water. They drank coffee while watching Nardwuar and talked about Cardi B.

She didn't really say anything, but she was there and that was half the battle, wasn't it? The only thing she could think to say was that after drinking the coffee, her heart did not explode.

Her phone chimed and it was a Twitter DM from John's girlfriend. She had found him dead in his apartment. Suicide. His parents did not want her to tell anyone. She didn't know whether they were embarrassed about the way he died or that writers might god forbid contact them to give their condolences. Zoe knew it was a fucked-up mixture of both and that it was John's parents' hatred of his writing that caused him to feel a lot of shame.

Two days before she left for the poetry readings he told her he didn't want to be a writer anymore. Two days into the readings he messaged her but she never responded. She thought he just wanted to talk and that she could catch him when she got home to Chicago. A place where the best and worst things happened to her.

She would never be able to respond. Never know what he wanted. The only thing she could do when she got back to the city was look at all of their last messages and see where she went wrong. What she might have missed. Her boyfriend said there was nothing she could do and then he ran out to get her food because he was so concerned. Zoe was broken and her cat Minion sat with her while he ran out because her cat was equally concerned. While waiting, she drank coffee she took home from Miami and finally felt like her heart could explode.

She went into Dropbox and stared at the last poem she wrote with John over and over again until the words lost all meaning. It was called "Here the Cat Saves the Day."

This was that poem:

i am at work

lots of people are at work

you will talk about work again and then you will die

eventually

everyone is at work and nobody is noticing anything

there is something occurring at an incredible distance and you are always where you'd rather not be

small animals are beginning to disappear in first unknown and later record quantities

there is a staggering catastrophe and it is recurring every 3-5 minutes and there is nothing compelling occurring in your life

if you were forced to write a meaningful statement at gunpoint you'd probably write something like 'pretty sure i'm vanishing at the speed of the rest of my life'

if you think about world history incredible things happening over massive time frames that are generally indifferent to worldviews and personal belief systems are shaping dozens of topics and worldviews and even person to person communication that may not find expression in any relatively meaningful period of time in terms of human civilization or biological life

i'm not convinced ratiocination on long term timescales could have been selected for

in a better world i am going to email part of myself to you

and toward the end of the day on a friday you will stare in the direction of a suspension bridge that you drive by every day after work and you will feel like a tiny mouse cursor moving in that direction but you will continue to move and you won't meet the edge of the screen of the rest of your life that you normally run into before moving back to the same point you were at the day before when you felt compelled to obviate your sense of personhood in the silent promise and comfort of dreamless sleep which you have not experienced in any rejuvenating sense since at least when you were in college coming home on the weekends to your parents' house

stock prices are changing and you don't want to think about another long day in the office

you can't conceptualize life without being in the office

when everyone else is enjoying refreshing beverages you are diving headfirst into the theoretical end of your life

which you feel like you have been watching on a daily basis in slow motion on repeat for at least fifteen years

developments in information technology do not take your mind off this

you are beginning to measure your life in terms of how many cats you've owned by the end of a life you might have had seven cats

you will be seven cats old when you stop going to work and start listening to repeats of the end of your life which you have been actively trying to avoid thinking about since you were at least fifteen

over the suspension bridge of Portland there are clouds

and the clouds are sweeping and vast

and they are illuminated by all the colors of sunset in the month of July

and accidentally there is a feeling that escapes from the dimensions of color

and it engulfs you

and it is indifferent to world history or natural selection

and you are beginning to experience a positive sensation like petting the first cat you owned while the rest of the world dissipates and becomes cosmic background radiation that thoughtlessly sustains the very ebb and flow of life

you have stopped thinking about causality

trees in the summer swell in the breeze

cicada sounds

like fire

like the universe erupting with its own timeless agony

like a monolith of emotional reflexivity reiterating its duration of speechless wonder

like a germ of life in arctic environs

gestating beneath the faultless stars

like everything becoming a metaphor for its own fulfillment

you vanish like the sound of cicada

there is a new fire

the universe erupts with a metaphor of itself

a cat leaps

is this what is left

is this what we have

an accidental narrative...

Acknowledgements

Shouts out to Bulent, Hayley, Alyssa, and Starbuck. They constantly hyped me up and made me write this damn book. Coffee helped too.

To my ride or die friends. The 2am people who saved me from my worst self. You know who you are.

I am now no longer the only one living girl in Chicago.

About Mallory Smart

Mallory Smart is a Chicago-based writer and is the Editor-in-Chief of the publishing house, Maudlin House. She also talks about music and literature on the podcast, *Textual Healing.*

OTHER VERY FINE TITLES FROM
TRIDENT PRESS

Blood-Soaked Buddha/Hard Earth Pascal
by Noah Cicero

it gets cold
by jasper avery

Major Diamonds Nights & Knives
by Katie Foster

Cactus
by Nathaniel Kennon Perkins

The Pocket Emma Goldman

Sixty Tattoos I Secretly Gave Myself at Work
by Tanner Ballengee

The Pocket Peter Kropotkin

The Silence is the Noise
by Bart Schaneman

The Pocket Aleister Crowley

*Propaganda of the Deed:
The Pocket Alexander Berkman*

Los Espiritus
by Josh Hyde

The Soul of Man Under Socialism
by Oscar Wilde

www.tridentcafe.com/trident-press-titles

Printed in the USA
CPSIA information can be obtained
at www.ICGtesting.com
JSHW082059100823
46348JS00002B/137